Aliens on Vacation

Aliens on Vacation

by Clete Barrett Smith

illustrated by Christian Slade

SCHOLASTIC INC.
New York Toronto London Auckland
Sydney Mexico City New Delhi Hong Kong

ISBN 978-0-545-44736-2

Text copyright © 2011 by Clete Barrett Smith.
Illustrations copyright © 2011 by Christian Slade. All rights reserved.
Published by Scholastic Inc., 557 Broadway, New York, NY 10012, by
arrangement with Hyperion Books for Children, an imprint of Disney Book
Group, LLC. SCHOLASTIC and associated logos are trademarks
and/or registered trademarks of Scholastic Inc.

12 11 10 9 8 7 6 5 4 3 2   12 13 14 15 16 17/0

Printed in the U.S.A.   40

First Scholastic printing, January 2012

For Myra,
always

1

When the taxi pulled up to Grandma's place, I wanted to burrow under the seat and cower in shame. I blinked a few times, but the view didn't get any better. Of all the places my parents had dumped me for a summer, this was the dumpiest.

The sign out front said it all: THE INTERGALACTIC BED AND BREAKFAST. The three-story Victorian home had at least the *potential* to be normal, with its white picket fence and rocking chairs on the wraparound porch, but... no. The house was jet black, with huge murals of comets and stars and planets on each side, painted on with what looked like glittery nail polish.

I wondered if I would have to submit a formal application to be the town freak, or if being related to Grandma meant I would be automatically awarded the title.

The taxi driver filled his stubbly cheeks with air and blew it out as he studied the front entrance. "This has gotta be the place, kid."

"Yep," I said.

He scratched his jowls with the back of his hand. "You know, I saw a documentary one time about the nut jobs who obsess over those old *Star Trek* shows. 'Trekkies.' This one guy, a dentist, he decorated his office like that ship . . . whaddaya call it? . . . oh yeah, the *Enterprise*. Even made his assistants wear these crazy space uniforms." He looked at the crowd of silver spaceship sculptures on Grandma's lawn. "Is this one of those kinds of places?"

"Yep," I said.

He was quiet for a moment. Then he said, "Those people are kind of weird."

"Yep," I said.

Muttering to himself, the driver pushed his door open and walked to the trunk to grab my suitcase. I stayed in the back of the taxi, not ready to accept the fact that I had to spend the next two months, three days, and fourteen hours of my life here.

The place was a dead end. Just past Grandma's fence the asphalt gave out, and the street turned into a narrow road of mud and gravel, twisting up into the hills to disappear into the forest. A mile or so back, the sign at the entrance to the town had read: WELCOME TO FOREST GROVE, WASHINGTON: YOUR OASIS IN THE WILDERNESS. They sure got the wilderness part right.

My mind churned with escape fantasies. I could make friends with the driver and stay in the taxi as he shuttled tourists around all summer. I could sleep in the trunk and buy meals from gas station vending machines. I bet he'd even let me drive once in a while, maybe at night, out on the country roads with no cops around. Then we could—

The daydream died when the taxi driver wrenched my door open with a screech of rusted metal. "All right, fella, you can sit there all day if you want. But I'll have to start charging you by the hour."

I willed my legs to push me out of the taxi, then dug into the pocket of my jeans for some cash. After carefully counting out a thick wad of ones and fives, I realized that I was blowing almost half the money my parents had given me for the summer just on the taxi ride. I double-checked the fare meter, worried that maybe the driver was charging too much, taking advantage of a kid traveling alone. But I shook it off. After all, it had taken over two hours to get here from the airport, every minute of travel time sucking me deeper into the wilderness. This whole state was nothing but trees and mountains. They probably had to do some heavy logging this morning just to clear out a space for my airplane to land.

The driver grabbed my cash, took one more look at the Intergalactic Bed and Breakfast, and shook his head. "Lotsa luck, kid," he said before slamming the door and driving away.

I stared at Grandma's place and snorted. There had already been lotsa luck for me since school let out for the summer last week. It had all been bad luck.

I thought this was going to be the first summer that I actually got to stay home. But Mom had a last-minute business trip to Jacksonville to lead one of her management seminars for corporate honchos. And Dad had to help one of his partners in the law firm get a new office up and running in Atlanta.

They could have dished out a little extra cash for our housekeeper to stay at our place full-time for the summer. I spend enough time with her anyway. Or, since I'm old enough now, they could have let me crash with friends. Heck, for a chance to be closer to home I could have survived another stay with Mom's sister and her annoying little kids in Lakeland (like the summer after fourth grade) or even another two-month sentence confined to the smelly cabins of the Happy Camper Sleepaway Adventure (summer after fifth grade).

But instead they shipped me out of Tampa, Florida, and all the way across the country to stay with Dad's mom. We had never been out here to visit before, but that wasn't too unusual; my parents don't really travel unless it's for work.

I walked toward the front gate, kicking a little too hard at rocks in my path and looking up at my bizarre prison for the summer. How was I supposed to make the seventh grade all-star basketball team now? Coach set up summer practices three times a week and tournaments almost every weekend. I was finally going to have the chance to show him I could play point guard better than Tyler Sandusky. Everyone knows that Coach figures out the starting lineup during the summer schedule. The official tryouts in the winter only last two days, and they're a joke.

Now Tyler would win our bet on which one of us will

be in the starting five, and I'd have to fork over a month's allowance. In fact, I'd be lucky to even make the team as a bench-gargoyle, just sitting there and watching Tyler play. More likely I'd be back on the intramural squad, playing with the other rejects who didn't make the real team, while Tyler traveled all over Hillsborough County with the all-stars, competing against the other middle schools. Some of those bigger schools even have cheerleaders.

Not that it would make much difference to Mom or Dad, since they're usually too busy to come to my games. They barely looked up from their suitcases as I pled my case for being able to stay home and play ball this summer. Maybe even start lifting some weights. I doubted that a fully-equipped weight room was on the amenity list for an Intergalactic Bed and Breakfast.

"Success is a by-product of a well-trained mind. The body is much less important," my mom had said, neatly folding the fourth navy blue business suit to go in her luggage. "Set goals, and then envision incremental steps for success each day to achieve your objective." Nice advice, Mom. That was probably line 4, paragraph 3b of her corporate training seminar brochure, and somehow I don't think Coach had read that one. Dad's response was about as helpful. He just cleared his throat and said that some things were more important than sports.

So I supposed I might as well forget about hoops and join the Sci-Fi/Fantasy Club. There were no tryouts for that one, just a willingness to give up any hope of appearing normal and fitting in at school. Those guys (and I do mean *guys*—no cheerleader would be caught dead, alive, or zombie at one of their events) dressed up in costumes and ran around with foam swords and plastic laser guns. In public. They even learned to speak languages that didn't exist, like Klingon or Elvish. (I have enough trouble with Intro to Spanish.) Sure, they looked like they were having fun, but...was it worth making such geeks of themselves?

As I studied Grandma's place, I realized it must cater to people like that after they've grown up, a place to escape the old nine-to-five and relive those Sci-Fi/Fantasy Club glory days. Should be a real interesting bunch to hang out with this summer.

It was hard to tell it was summer at all, here. It couldn't have been more than sixty-five degrees, the temperature on Christmas Day back home. Not a scrap of blue sky anywhere, the thick layer of clouds so low it seemed like it was being propped up by all of those trees.

A sheriff's car cruised down the street, and the driver stared at me as he passed. A wide-brimmed hat cast a shadow over his round face, partially obscuring his frown and bushy mustache. A toothpick jutted out the side of his mouth. His gaze stayed fixed on me as he drove by.

Just past Grandma's place he pulled a wide U-turn, tires splashing through the mud puddles of the dirt road, then headed back to town. Must be a pretty pathetic small town if the arrival of a single outsider is cause for a law enforcement drive-by.

The door to Grandma's place opened up then. The person who stepped out made the whole scene even more bizarre.

He was at least seven feet tall and so impossibly skinny

that his shabby thrift-store suit looked like it was draped over a hanger and walking around by itself. The sleeves were way too short, and the arms that flopped out were the gray color of dying fish.

He scanned the road, neck on a swivel, the skin stretched over his gaunt face the same dead-fish hue as his arms. Then in three giant strides he was down the porch steps, across the front walkway, and standing on the other side of the fence from me.

He bent in half at the waist, lowering his head until his gray carrot of a nose was touching the mailbox. With short wet doggy sniffs, he smelled the mailbox all over.

He straightened back up and looked at me. He squinched his eyes and tilted his head, like maybe he was trying to remember something. Finally, he grabbed the brim of his old-man fedora with both hands, lifted it straight off his head, and nodded once at me.

Okay ... I wasn't too sure how I was supposed to respond to that, so I just sort of waved a little.

Then he jammed his hat back on his gray, bald head, stepped over the fence, and took off down the sidewalk. Five more strides with those beanpole legs, and he was halfway down the street toward town.

What? I knew a place like the Intergalactic Bed and Breakfast would attract some oddball types, but still ...

I opened the gate and saw a small notebook lying on the ground. Had the tall guy dropped it? I picked it up and flipped through the first couple of pages. They looked something like this:

I knew it. The journal was like something one of the sci-fi/fantasy guys would put together. I wondered which imaginary language this guy was learning.

I tucked the journal into my carry-on bag and lugged it and my suitcase down the walkway.

Click! Click!

I stopped, looked around. Didn't see anything.

I switched the heavy suitcase to my other hand and kept walking.

Click!

There! Close, in the bushes, a camera sticking out from the green leaves.

"Hey!" I shouted, dropping my suitcase. The branches shuddered, and the mysterious photographer shot out from the bushes, jumped the side fence, and disappeared into the forest. I could just make out that the person was about my height; but my only clear glimpse was a yellow baseball cap with a long ponytail sticking out, bouncing with each step.

I had hoped there might be some people my age around here...but not if they were going to hide in the bushes and take pictures.

So what was I dealing with here? A suspicious sheriff, a mailbox-sniffer, and small-town paparazzi. "This place sure has quite the welcoming committee."

I sighed. Did talking to myself mean I was going crazy, or just that being blood-related to the person who owned this place meant that weirdness was carving out a genetic foothold in my behavior? Either way, not a real good sign.

I finally reached the porch. The welcome mat was decorated with clusters of stars grouped together to spell out ALL ARE WELCOME WHO COME IN PEACE.

An old-timey brass knocker in the shape of a smiley-face moon hung in the middle of the door. I lifted it and let it crash against the door a couple of times. A muffled cry from inside the house sounded like it could have been "Come in."

This was it. I had tried everything to get out of this— begging, negotiating, hiding, praying—but none of it had worked, and now I was actually here. I took a deep breath, grabbed the doorknob, and got ready to start getting it over with.

2

When I was a kid I used to read superhero comic books. But most people in middle school think those are immature, so I've stepped up to graphic novels now.

But I still sneak in a superhero comic occasionally, usually when Marvel runs their alternate reality stories, called the What If...? series. For example, *What If Spider-Man Joined the Fantastic Four?* or *What If Wolverine Were Lord of the Vampires?*

These mash-ups make for fun storylines...but the effect was a little more unsettling in real life. I opened the door to Grandma's place, and it looked like someone had tried to answer the question *What If 1967 Met 2167?*

I expected the space-age stuff, of course. *Star Wars* movie posters on the walls, mobiles of planets and constellations dangling from the ceiling, that sort of thing.

But it all looked so much stranger for being a mash-up with the hippie era. The front door opened onto a sitting room where outer space mingled with the spaced out: lava lamps, fat wine bottle candleholders in wicker casings, strings of multicolored beads dangling from furniture made of driftwood. A wisp of incense smoke drifted across a stained-glass picture of all the planets in the solar system, only in this version the sun was a giant peace sign.

The entire universe was still celebrating the Summer of Love at Grandma's place.

I couldn't believe that my dad the corporate lawyer had grown up here. But it was getting easier to see why he'd never been back.

And then I saw Grandma. Dad had e-mailed her some pictures of me. But I think that she hadn't really figured out the mysterious workings of the computer, so we didn't usually get many of her sent back to us. But I had seen a few that she had snail-mailed, so I recognized her.

And I noticed the same thing in person that I did in those pictures: she sure didn't look old enough to be someone's grandma. Her hair wasn't squashed up in a gray bun on top of her head or anything: it was blond, and really long. It was parted in the middle and it framed her face, dropping all the way to her waist in waves. And she didn't really have many wrinkles. Maybe all that peace and love had been good to her.

By the way she was dressed, it was obvious she did the decorating around here. She wore a loose, earth-toned tunic-thingy that fell to her knees, printed with swirling colors, like one of those abstract works of art that look like a little kid painted it. She wore wool socks with sandals made out of corkboard-looking material, and she was draped in dozens of bamboo necklaces and bracelets. Dad must have acquired his taste for three-piece suits after he went off to law school.

Grandma saw me at the door and glided over to me. Her glasses were tinted pink, and the oversized lenses made her eyes look really big. "Welcome back, young traveler," she said. Her voice was soft and she pronounced each word separately. "I don't think I remember your GRADE. It's been so busy around here lately."

My *grade*? Did we have to start there? It's supposed to be summer vacation. "Well, I just finished sixth and I'm going into..."

Before I could finish, she put her soft hands on my face. It wasn't like a typical distant relative pinching a kid's cheeks at Thanksgiving dinner; it was more like she was...I don't know, *tugging* at them. And she studied my face really closely. Weird. But maybe she was trying to find some family resemblance. I sure hoped she didn't.

Grandma let go and shook her head. "No, I'm afraid I don't remember your GRADE at all. But you look fantastic. Very natural."

"Ummm...thanks?" I said. She must have meant healthy. My dad had said she was into organic food and that kind of stuff. What else could I expect at a place like this?

Grandma looked past me, out the door and down the

street. "I'm searching for another one of my guests. I wonder if you've seen him? He's quite tall." She stretched her arm up over her head as high as she could. "And he looks sort of . . . well, grayish, you could say." She frowned slightly. "Wait. Not grayish. That sounds rather odd, doesn't it? I probably shouldn't say that out loud. I meant 'ashen.' That's it, his skin is quite ashen."

"Long nose?" I said. "Dark suit?"

Her eyes shone behind her pink glasses. "That's him exactly. You've seen him, then? Oh, I'm so pleased." She kept looking at me, standing very still, like maybe I was going to pull that tall guy out of my pocket.

"He just left," I said.

"Oh, I do hope he's not frightened," she said. "Such a gentle creature." She pushed her bamboo bracelets up her forearm to read her watch. "I really should go and look for him, but there's just so much to do around here." She seemed to be talking to herself, so I didn't say anything.

I suddenly smelled something bitter. "Is something burning?" I asked.

"Heaven and Earth!" she cried, hustling down the hall, her tunic fluttering behind her. She flung open the swinging door to the kitchen. A clanging of pots and pans was followed by cold water hitting hot metal with that *pssshhh* sound.

Finally, she reappeared in the doorway, wiping her hands on a dish towel and shaking her head. "A total loss, I'm afraid. So much for my famous tofu-and-squash stuffing with brown rice and wild mushrooms." She sighed. "All of this has become a bit too much for a one-woman show." She stretched out both arms to indicate the entire bed-and-breakfast. "Especially when that one woman gets a little bit older each year." She tilted her head and studied me. "But please, forgive my poor manners. May I help you? I assume you have been out visiting the town with your parents. Will they be back soon?"

"No. No, it's me. Scrub, er—David." I wasn't sure which name Dad had told her. Scrub is a pretty embarrassing name, obviously, but I couldn't even remember the last time someone called me David.

She just kept looking at me.

"You know . . . your grandson," I said. Man, she was even spacier than the decorations.

Her eyes got round again. "But you weren't supposed to be here until Tuesday."

"Well . . . I'm pretty sure that it *is* Tuesday." Apparently there were no Earth calendars on Planet New Age Hippie.

Grandma got a confused, faraway look in her eyes. Then she counted on her fingers and muttered something to herself that didn't quite sound like English. Finally she snapped out of it. "How swiftly spins the wheel of the cosmos. Tuesday already." She shook her head and that long hair waved back and forth. "I've been so busy lately that the days have raced by without stopping to say hello properly."

She looked at me and smiled again. "Oh, but it's really you, then? How wonderful." She threw both arms around me in a bear hug. She could really squeeze hard for someone with such skinny arms. I just kind of stood there. We're not bear-huggers in my family. Not really human-huggers, either. "Please forgive me. I told you all of this was too much for a one-woman show."

Grandma stopped the hugging and stepped back, holding

my face in her hands. This time it felt more normal. "But enough about my troubles; let's get a good gander at you." She peered at me through her pink lenses. "It's a handsome young man you are, well and truly. Starting to look just like your father. Can't believe I didn't notice it before." She stared at me like she was trying to memorize my face. It was a different feeling, to be looked at so carefully. Back home, everyone was so busy with their own stuff that I sort of felt invisible sometimes. Which was fine with me.

Grandma was really smiling now, all of her teeth showing and her eyes bunched up. "Of course, the last time I saw you was at your first birthday party, so I guess it's a good thing you've grown so much." She laughed at her little joke. "And your name was David then, but now you go by . . . Scrub? That's a colorful nickname. How did you get it?"

Second grade. Our class production of *Robin Hood*. All the kids who didn't want speaking parts—like me—were dressed up as trees. Except I was pretty short in grade school, and my mom had made the costume too small, so I was about half the size of the other trees. And on opening night, Tyler Sandusky's older brother was in the front row. When I went onstage he said, loud enough for everyone in the first five rows to hear, "It's supposed to be Sherwood Forest, not Sherwood Scrub Brush." All of his stupid friends laughed. Tyler was there, and he laughed, too. Anyway, the name just kind of stuck. What also stuck was my determination never to open myself up to that kind of embarrassment again.

"Oh, it's not a nickname. It's just . . . you know, something that everyone calls me."

"Well, I like it," Grandma said. "And I'm a woman who

understands the need to choose a title for yourself. When I went off to college I told everyone that my name was Sun-shine. No one has called me Vernus Mae since, and thank the Creator for that." She finally let go of my face. "Is Scrub what I shall call you?"

I shrugged. "I guess." At least I was used to it.

"You can simply call me Grandma, if you don't mind. I think I'd rather like that."

"Okay."

"Now, after your big day of travel, I suppose you'd like something hot to eat before I start peppering you with more questions. I could sauté some gluten squares in soy sauce, and I think there's some spinach salad left over, an offering fresh from the soil of Mother Earth—I have a vegetable garden right in the backyard."

Yikes. Not really what I'm used to. Back home, a delivery service drops off a load of "gourmet" frozen entrées the first Friday of each month. The chest freezer in the garage is full of them. Mom still writes out a note with the microwave instructions every morning and evening, even though I've been heating them up myself since about second grade.

Grandma must have read my expression. "Or perhaps a bit of organic couscous with cucumber slices?"

Oh, boy. I hope this town is at least big enough to have a McDonald's. "Um, thanks, but actually I just need to use the bathroom, if you don't mind."

"Of course. Let me show you where—" Grandma was interrupted by several sounds. First, a door slammed upstairs, then a teakettle whistled and the phone rang, and then there was, I don't know, kind of a wet *squelching* sound coming in through one of the windows. Grandma tried to look in four directions at once. "Great Galaxies, never a dull moment these days. I'm sorry—"

"It's okay, I'm sure I can find it."

Grandma smiled at me. "A fine young man and a charmer, Scrub, I can tell. It will be so good to have you here this summer." She opened a cupboard and plucked one of several keys hanging from hooks. "Here you go. Room Two-C, upstairs. Settle in and make yourself comfortable. There's a bathroom up there as well." The phone rang again and the teakettle whistle became a screech. Something thumped upstairs. Grandma glided away, calling to me over her shoulder. "Sorry to run. I'll check in with you soon."

Then she was gone, pushing through the swinging door into the kitchen. I grabbed my suitcase and hauled it up the hardwood staircase.

The halls were long and narrow, with high ceilings. The space theme continued up here, every guest room door bordered by gray plastic panels with all kinds of fakey-looking knobs and switches, like they were supposed to be portals on a spaceship or something. Atop each door was a theme sign: WELCOME TO THE MILKY WAY! or BLAST OFF TO THE ASTEROID BELT!

I set down my suitcase in front of room 2C (THE ANDROMEDA EXPRESS!), then looked for the bathroom. I stopped at the first door without a room number. I knocked softly and called "Hello?" before easing the door open a crack.

Whoa. There was something that looked kind of like a public men's room urinal... but it was mounted on the *ceiling*. The sink was really low, practically on the ground. The claw-foot bathtub was tilted at a forty-five-degree angle and filled with what looked like super-foamy pink shaving cream.

And the mess. Purple slime oozed out of the ceiling-urinal in long, goopy ropes, and an orange puddle with bright blue polka dots seeped out from under the sink.

I had had to go to the bathroom pretty bad for over an hour, but I wasn't even sure where I would start in here. Maybe this was taking the space theme a little too far?

Grandma appeared behind me. "Oh, I'm sorry, Scrub, that's supposed to be locked." She grabbed the knob and shut the door. "That's not a . . . well, that's not a bathroom for *you*. Try the next door." She nodded toward the adjacent door as she hurried down the hall and up the next staircase.

3

When I stepped out of the bathroom, there was a family of five approaching from the other end of the hall. On all fours. Seriously. All of them, the parents and the kids, were bear-walking down the hall, studying the floor like Sherlock Holmes.

I scrunched up against the wall to give them room to pass, and walked quickly toward my room.

The dad stopped and looked up at me, turning his head this way and that as I tried to rush by. He was wearing a huge pair of sunglasses, almost as big as those oversized novelty glasses you can win at carnival games. "Of course," he said in a booming voice that was too loud for the hallway. I froze. He grunted and pushed himself upright, then helped his wife and kids to their feet. "This is the way it is done here," he bellowed at his family. "Remember for the outside."

They all stood on shaky legs, trying to stay balanced. Each family member wore a matching pair of those enormous sunglasses. The kids kept toppling over and the dad hoisted them upright again.

When they had all managed to stay balanced for a few moments, they smiled and gave me double-armed waves before tottering drunkenly down the hall, arms outstretched to prevent them from crashing into the walls.

I stayed very still until they rounded the corner, then hurried down to room 2C with my suitcase, fumbled with the room key, and closed the door firmly behind me. Man, this place was even weirder than I expected.

I leaned back, letting the door support my weight. Could all of this be chalked up to the sci-fi oddball clientele? It seemed like...I don't know, like something else.

Maybe it was Washington State. After all, this was over three thousand miles from home. And these people lived in the wilderness. Things were bound to be different here.

And then there was Canada. We were only a few miles from the border. I didn't know much about Canadian culture, if there was such a thing. Maybe being so close, some of their customs had leaked across the international border, like osmosis.

My eyes had been mindlessly drifting across the room as I came up with theories, but suddenly a terrible realization pulled me out of my thoughts.

Room 2C had no TV.

The space where the TV should have been, but was not, was enormous. I shifted my gaze all around the room, like maybe the TV was playing hide-and-seek.

Then a truly horrible thought occurred to me. I opened my laptop and booted it up. I hit the "Connect to Internet" icon, and fifteen agonizing seconds later, got the dreaded news: *No Wireless Connection Available*. I checked my cell phone. No bars.

How much worse could this summer possibly get?

I think up until that moment I had been holding out hope that things could somehow work out.

My shoulders slumped. When I dumped my clothes out of my suitcase, it felt like an admission of defeat, like I was officially surrendering any chance I had for a fun, or at least somewhat normal, summer.

Something mounted on the wall caught my eye, a bronze plaque with the following message:

House Rules for a Successful Visit

1. Leave nothing behind
2. Take nothing with you
3. Dress appropriately
4. Two arms, two legs, one head
5. No harming the natives

What? How could number four even be considered a rule? And *No harming the natives???* Did that mean Native Americans? I had seen signs for Indian reservations on the bus ride here—Tulalip, Swinomish, Nooksack, Lummi—but I couldn't imagine there would be a problem with people "harming" them on vacation.

I shook my head, as if that would help clear my mind of everything I had seen. I didn't want to get sucked into thinking about any of it. What went on here was none of my business anyway. If these people wanted a hokey outer-space adventure for their vacation, then let them throw their money away. As soon as I got out of here I wouldn't have to think about it ever again.

When my suitcase was empty I tried to stash it in the closet, but the door was locked. Everything else in this house was made of wood, but the closet door was a dull metallic color. Instead of a doorknob it had one of those big handles, like you see on heavy exterior doors at schools or office buildings. I jerked on it, but the door didn't budge.

I wondered if all the rooms were like this, or if Grandma just didn't want me to mess with whatever she had stored in there. That would figure. Old people never really trust people my age. They're always looking at kids suspiciously, even when we're not doing anything wrong.

I dropped my suitcase in the corner and just threw my clothes on top of it in a big pile. I wasn't too worried about the mess. It's not like my mom was going to show up anytime soon, and she never really noticed what my bedroom was like anyway.

After that I opened up the window. Dusk had fallen and the air that flowed in was cool, raising goose bumps on my arms, but it was better than the stuffiness of the room.

While I looked over the front lawn, that sheriff's car drove up again and parked out front. The sheriff stepped out, a big man with a round belly, and opened the car's rear door. He pulled out the tall gray man in the old suit, then marched him up the walkway, stretching to hold him above the elbow like a principal taking an oversized kid to the office.

I left my room and hustled along the corridor and down the stairs. Grandma was already at the door. The sheriff stood on the porch, his meaty hand still clamped on the tall guy. I hid behind a lamp and spied on the conversation.

"—so sorry, Sheriff Tate. You have my assurances I'll keep a better eye out," Grandma was saying.

"I've had plenty of your assurances lately," Sheriff Tate said. "How many times am I going to have to escort him back here? And more and more of your customers have been causing problems in town lately."

"Causing problems? I hardly think so."

"This one talks so's I could hardly understand him."

"I'm afraid that is not his fault. He is a foreigner and new to our language. Some people, Sheriff Tate, are aware of a world that exists outside of Forest Grove." The sheriff turned red and started to say something at that, but Grandma cut him off. "Thank you for your time. Knowing how very busy you are, I extend to you all my sympathies. We won't inconvenience you further." She pulled Gray Man by the hand, but the sheriff kept his grip.

"I'm afraid it's a mite more than an inconvenience," Tate said, obviously straining to keep up the show of politeness. "It's also about public safety, ma'am."

"Public safety?" Grandma said. "Was he doing something illegal?"

"Well...no, not exactly." Tate cleared his throat. "But he was acting pretty strange. He was walking around the park, and...well, he was smelling things."

"I see," Grandma said. "And are there rules about smelling things in the park? Perhaps a new city ordinance I am not aware of?"

"No, there's no law against smelling things at the park." Tate glanced around the porch and suddenly looked uncomfortable. "But I...well, I guess I was worried about the children down there. They might have been spooked."

"Of course," Grandma said. "We must protect the children. Now, if you'll excuse us, I need to show him to his room." She pulled more firmly on Gray Man's hand. Finally, Tate released his grip, and Grandma yanked him inside.

Tate pointed his ragged toothpick at Grandma. The thin layer of politeness died. "I'm getting tired of this. If I need to come back here one more time, I'm going to—"

"I'm sure that won't be necessary, thank you." She shut the door. Right in his face. Grandma was a little tougher than I would have given her credit for.

She led Gray Man to an easy chair and motioned for him to sit. She patted him on the back of his hand. "I hope that man didn't frighten you."

The tall man's eyes got squinty and his mouth scrunched up, like he was puzzling through something. It was a minute or so before he said, "I hold... much regret feeling. And the shame. Please to feel... forgiveness inside of you. For my actions." His voice was gravelly and liquidy at the same time.

Grandma smiled at him. "Of course, dear. Don't you worry about that sheriff one bit." She kept patting his hand. "Everyone deserves a nice, peaceful vacation, don't they? And everyone deserves to be treated well, no matter how different they appear."

Gray Man finally lifted his head and spotted me standing in the corner. "Ah. This little man... I had a meeting with him before-time."

Grandma turned. "Well, hello, Scrub! I didn't see you there. Please say hello to Mr. Harnox. He's visiting with us."

"Hi," I said. Mr. Harnox nodded, but he still looked miserable after his encounter with the sheriff. I could relate—I'd be pretty freaked out if some cop were that mad at me, too. The gray man lowered his head and held it in his hands.

Suddenly I remembered something that might cheer him up. I crossed to where I had left my carry-on bag by the front door and pulled out the weird-looking journal. I took a few steps toward Mr. Harnox. "Excuse me, but is this yours? I found it outside when you left."

The tall man lifted his head, and his eyes got really big. I think maybe he was trying to smile, but it was hard to tell, because his lips went kind of crooked, and his teeth were small and sharp and really far apart, so that was distracting. "Oh, many thanks and thanks of plenty to the little man."

Mr. Harnox grabbed the journal in one hand, then looked at his other hand for a moment before slowly stretching it out to me. I think he wanted me to shake it. He had these long, skeletal fingers that were constantly gnarling them-selves into weird shapes. I shuddered a little, but hoped he didn't notice. I didn't want to be rude, so I forced myself to reach out and give him a quick shake. His hands were sort of moist and squishy.

I quickly let go and looked up to see Grandma beaming at me. "That was very kind of you, Scrub. I know that Mr. Harnox's journal is very important to him." The gray man bobbed his head happily in agreement. "And after that unpleas-ant little visit from the sheriff, it's such a comfort to know that there are those who can make others feel welcome here. I appreciate your helping to restore my faith in humanity."

I shrugged. That seemed a bit much for giving some guy a journal and shaking his hand. "No problem. Man, that sheriff was really hassling you."

"Oh, no matter. I've handled worse than him in my day," Grandma said. She patted Mr. Harnox on the shoulder. "I'll fix you something to eat. Would you care to join us, Scrub?"

"I'll probably just go to bed. I'm still on East Coast time."

"Okay, but wait one moment before you go." Grandma led Mr. Harnox through the swinging door into the kitchen, then reappeared and came over to me.

"Is that guy okay?" I said.

"Why do you ask?"

I shrugged. "I don't know. He looks a little . . . you know?"

Grandma sighed. "Oh, poor Mr. Harnox. It's probably time to wash that suit again. He's been here over two years, after all."

"*Two years?* At a bed-and-breakfast?"

"Yes, I'm afraid he can't go home. He's . . . well, he's a bit trapped."

I started to ask what she meant, but Grandma leaned in close and dropped her voice to a whisper. "Scrub, do you think you could do me a favor?"

"Sure."

She glanced at the kitchen door, then back at me. "Did you happen to get a look at the house rules when you were settling in?"

"Um . . . yeah. Yeah, I did."

She stepped even closer, her voice so low I could hardly hear it. "Could you keep your eyes open, let me know if you see any of the Tourists breaking a rule?"

Sure, Grandma, I thought. *The moment I see one of your customers attack a tribe of Native Americans, you'll be the first to know.*

The skepticism must have made its way into my face, because she laughed and said, "I'm sorry, Scrub. I've been running this place for so long it all seems routine to me. Nothing much surprises anymore." She used both hands to clear the hair out of her eyes, then whispered again. "My guests are . . . well, you could say, they are *foreign* to the area . . . and the rules help to protect them."

I nodded. Slowly. "Okay . . ."

"Oh, that doesn't help much, does it?" Grandma fidgeted with her hands. "It's just I've never—"

Dishes clattered and crashed behind the kitchen door. "Oh dear," she said. "No time now." She grabbed my hands and looked into my eyes. "Please just let me know if you see anyone breaking the rules."

She was looking at me so seriously, staring right at me with big round eyes, so I answered seriously. "Yeah. No problem."

"Oh, that's such a relief. It is truly a blessing to have you here," Grandma said, rushing toward the kitchen door. "Thanks again, Scrub." She disappeared into the kitchen.

"You're welcome," I called after her. I still had no idea what she was talking about.

4

I woke up in the middle of the night with no idea
where I was until a rush of cold air and the splatter
of rain against the house clued me in. I was freezing,
even under all of these thick quilts. I usually sleep
under a single sheet back in Tampa.

I climbed out of bed, and after tugging the window closed, I raced to get back under the covers. But
before I could shut my eyes, I noticed something.

There was a blue circle the size of a dinner plate
glowing in the center of that big metallic closet door.
I rubbed the sleep out of my eyes and looked again.

Still there. It pulsed, getting a little brighter, then dimming. A faint thrumming faded in and out in time with the glowing.

I shivered. Only, I don't think that had much to do with the cold night air. To be honest, I wanted to pull the covers over my head and forget all about that thing.

But that was stupid. After all of the crazy things I'd done when Tyler Sandusky dared me, all our bets and competitions, checking out this closet door seemed pretty tame. And besides, I was going to officially be a teenager soon, and teenagers—not to mention potential starting point guards on the all-star team—did not let things like this freak them out.

I finally talked myself into slipping out of bed.

I knelt in front of the closet door, the circle at eye level. No letters or markings of any kind. Just clear blue light. I held my hand a few inches from it, testing it for heat, but didn't feel anything.

Finally, I closed the gap and placed my palm on the blue surface.

"Unauthorized," said a mechanical voice, and it startled me so badly I fell backward. The blue light faded until it was completely gone.

I jumped back into bed, and this time I *did* pull the covers up over my head.

5

A different kind of weird light woke me next: sun-light. The cloud cover had actually broken up. Maybe there was some type of summer here after all. I glanced at the closet, but it was just a door. It was easy to believe that the blue circle—and that voice —had all been a dream.

I stared at the ceiling and wondered what I'd be doing if I were home. It was three hours later in Florida, so Tyler Sandusky and I would probably be down at the pool after morning basketball practice.

A bout of homesickness hit me like a weight on my chest, so heavy it was actually hard to breathe.

I grabbed my cell and checked the last text message Tyler had sent just before I left town: *good luck w/the Challenge. u r goin down, sucka!*

The Great Weekly Challenges. Tyler and I invented them two years ago. Past Challenges included Who Can Do the Scariest Thing (Me: riding my bike through the cemetery at midnight; Tyler: putting his tongue on a wasps' nest) and Who Can Do the Stupidest Thing (Me: throwing a water balloon at a group of high schoolers and running away; Tyler: sprinting across the driving range on Saturday morning when every retired person in Florida is smacking golf balls).

Challenges must be completed in one week. The prize for winning is not really that exciting: you just get to pick the next dare. But there is no backing down from a Challenge.

Since we wouldn't see each other this summer, the Great Weekly Challenges became the Colossal Summer Challenge. It was Tyler's turn to pick, and he came up with Who Will Be the First to Kiss a (Nonrelative) Girl.

I think he just made this one up because he'd already come pretty close to kissing Amanda Peterson, and he wanted an excuse to go ahead and try to do it. In some ways, Tyler's more like a brother than a friend. I mean, we've lived next door to each other since preschool, and just always hung out together. Even though he knew me better than anyone else, even my own parents, I was starting to wonder whether we'd even be friends if we met for the first time right now.

Anyway, I also think he made up this Challenge because he knew the closest I'd come to kissing anyone was when the girl playing Maid Marian in that Robin Hood play tripped, knocked me over in my tree costume, and fell right on top of me. The sequins on her dress got all tangled up with the leaves from my costume, so she was trapped there, flailing away and lying right on top of me, in front of a packed auditorium. It took five minutes for Little John and Friar Tuck to get her off me.

So Tyler knew I had no chance to win this Challenge. Besides, from what I'd seen so far, an Intergalactic Bed and Breakfast is not the best place to meet the ladies.

At least Tyler agreed to waive the video-confirmation requirement that we normally use to validate the winner. Without Internet or cell phone service, it was not like I could report back to him anyway. He'd probably won already.

My stomach rumbled. The last thing I had eaten was a packet of airplane peanuts too many hours ago. I pulled on jeans and a T-shirt and stepped into the hall, then trotted downstairs, where Grandma's customers milled around the sitting room.

It was a lot busier this morning. A couple sat on the couch, studying a map. They had pretty big heads but really short bodies. A woman, almost as tall as Mr. Harnox, studied the books on the highest bookshelf. A family of four, all very fat—almost entirely *round*, on second glance—were pulling on hiking boots by the front door. Everyone looked a little bit funny.

But I was too hungry to pay much attention to the customers. I walked into the kitchen to find Grandma at the stove, cooking something that looked like greenish oatmeal.

"Ah! A sweet and pleasant new day to you, Scrub."

"Morning."

The family from yesterday, with the shaky legs and over-sized sunglasses, was sitting at the big communal table eating breakfast. The dad got everyone's attention and jabbed his finger at me, smiling; then the entire family gave me double-armed waves from across the room. I lifted a hand in return. It was pretty embarrassing, since everyone else at the table had stopped eating to look at me too.

I turned to avoid all of those stares and found Grandma beaming at me. She gestured toward the table. "Those nice folks told me that you really helped them out yesterday, Scrub."

I shrugged. "Trust me, it really wasn't that big of a deal." I peeked over at the table, and the family was still smiling at me and flapping their arms so energetically it looked like they were trying to get the breakfast table to take flight.

"Well, you trust me, it meant the world and then some to them." Grandma poked me with her wooden spoon. "And I appreciate your being so kind to Mr. Harnox yesterday."

The kitchen door swung open and a lady walked in with a little kid. The polite term for the lady would be "big-boned" but, man, those would have to be some really big, round, squishy bones under there. The enormous dress she was wearing—more of a king-size bedsheet, actually—just barely covered all of that flesh.

She looked at Grandma and gestured to the kid, a boy who looked to be kindergarten-age with a miniature version of his mom's body. His faded Seattle Mariners baseball cap was about five sizes too big, and the bill drooped down to cover most of his face. "Is this head covering so necessary?"

the woman said. "He cannot see his own feet. He will be smashing into every things if we go to the outside like this."

Grandma made a sympathetic face. "It's truly sorry I am, ma'am. It was the smallest hat I could find this morning."

The lady looked upset at that. "This is not for acceptable." Her voice was getting a little too loud. Grandma glanced anxiously at the guests at the table. "I will not allow you to—"

"Maybe I can help," I said. I felt sort of bad for Grandma, not to mention the kid. I reached out to grab the hat. Grandma gasped a little and put her hand on my arm. She studied my face for a moment, then lowered her hand and nodded. I pulled the hat off the kid's head.

Whoa. Poor little guy. He must have had some kind of birth defect or something, because he was totally bald and he had these golf-ball-size lumps all over his head. I remembered seeing something on TV, maybe the Discovery Channel, about diseases that could affect little kids like that.

I could feel Grandma watching me, and I didn't want to embarrass the kid, so I kept my face as neutral as possible.

"Here you go," I said, trying to sound matter-of-fact. I turned the cap around and set it on his head backward, tucking the sides behind his ears so that it would stay in place. "There. You can see now, plus it looks better. That's the cool way to wear a cap."

The boy looked up at me. "Cool?"

"Yeah. It means *good*. You look good. The best."

The boy's smile was so big it threatened to split his round face in two. "Coo-oo-ool," he said.

The lady nodded once at me. "Thank you." She looked back at Grandma. "We go out now."

Grandma patted the boy on top of his baseball cap. "My wishes to you for a most enchanting day, travelers."

They pushed out through the swinging kitchen doors. Grandma turned to me, and she had a look in her eyes like maybe she was seeing me for the first time. "Scrub, I must say, it's a fine gift you have for dealing with my customers."

"Thanks." My face got a little warm. "Again, not really a big deal."

"Bigger than you think, maybe." She stirred the stuff in the pot. "Now, I'm sorry to make demands of you so early, especially since the jet lag must be making you exhausted, but I have a bit of a favor to ask you."

"No problem. What's up?" That family had at last stopped their waving, but it would still be nice to get out of the kitchen for a while.

"There are some things I desperately need at the grocery store." Grandma took off her glasses and wiped them on her apron. "It's a bit of a hike, but would you mind terribly going for me? You can borrow a grocery cart to bring back here, and I can return it later."

"All right." It might be fun to check out the town a little bit. There had to be at least a few kids my age around here.

And, okay, so maybe it was also a little bit nice to be asked. My parents never really asked for my help back home. Maybe to take the dog out or whatever, but not for something they really needed.

"That's wonderful. But please, enjoy a bit of breakfast before you go. You must be starving."

I looked at the bubbling mass of thick, greenish oatmeal.

"Um, that's okay," I said. A grocery story meant real food, like Pop-Tarts and frosted fruit pies and grape soda. My stomach rumbled at the thought.

A few minutes later I was out the front door and walking to town. Just after I passed the park, I ran into three guys. They were a couple of years older than me, maybe high schoolers. I tried not to seem too eager when I saw that one of them was bouncing a faded leather basketball.

I never know where to look when passing someone on the street. Seems weird to look straight ahead and avoid eye contact. But then again, you don't want to stare at someone and weird them out, either. I sort of looked down, and when they got close I lifted my head and tried the head-nod-with-raised-eyebrows combo, no smile, with some quick eye contact. I've seen other guys do that.

They stopped right in front of me. My mood perked up a little with the hope that they might ask me to play ball. Maybe this summer wouldn't be a total waste.

"Hey," said the one with the basketball.

"Hey."

"Where're you from?" said the tallest one.

"Florida."

By the way they looked at each other I could tell that wasn't the usual answer around here.

"That's cool," said the third one, a guy with blond hair. "You ever been to Disneyland?"

"It's Disney *World*, dork," the tall one said. "Disneyland's in California."

"Well, have you?"

That's the first question anyone asks when they hear you're from Florida. "Yeah. We only live a couple of hours away. We go all the time."

"Cool," said the guy with blond hair. "I'm Greg. This is Brian, and the big guy there is Eddie. We're gonna play ball at the park, but it gets boring with three people."

"Yeah," said Brian. "The only game you can play with three is cutthroat. You wanna come with and make it two-on-two?"

"Sure," I said, trying to act casual. "I just have to run to the store really quick, but I can meet you back here afterward."

"Nice," Greg said. "What's your name, anyway?"

I thought for a moment. *Scrub* is an especially brutal nickname for a baller, since it basically means second- or third-string. Now, I may not be the tallest guy in the world, but that doesn't necessarily matter when it comes to getting playing time. It's what I liked about being point guard: you can be the shortest guy and still be the leader of the team. Smarts are just as important as being athletic, maybe more.

I decided that being away from home could give me a fresh start. Today I would begin my new life as *David*. David the mysterious out-of-towner could be a great basketball player and someone the girls of Forest Grove lined up to kiss, Challenge or no Challenge. I opened my mouth to tell them my real name when—

"Yoo-hoo! Scrub! Wait a moment!"

My grandma. Headed our way, pedaling an ancient Schwinn with a big basket on the front of the handlebars. The basket had sunflower decorations all over it.

"You know the Space Place lady?" said Eddie.

"Wait—your name is *Scrub*?" said Brian.

"Yep," I said. I could feel my face getting red.

Grandma stepped off the bike and pulled a slip of paper out of her basket. "Here you go, Scrub. You forgot the grocery list." She smiled at the older guys. "Greetings to you on such a pleasant morning, gentlemen. I trust that you are happily and well met with my grandson?"

The guys didn't answer; they just looked at each other out of the corners of their eyes and smirked, just barely successful in not cracking up right in her face.

Grandma watched them. Sometimes old people can be clueless when it comes to reading teenagers.

When they still didn't say anything to her, Grandma glanced at me. "Oh, and one other thing, Scrub. Mr. Harnox is giving lessons on common courtesy this afternoon." She winked at me. "In case you know anyone who might benefit."

I had to stifle a groan. Her lame attempt to make fun of them went over their heads and just made her look more out of it.

She climbed back onto her bike. "Time to return home. I'm afraid the plants in my spice garden become rather cross with me when they don't get their drink of water first thing in the morning." She turned her bike around to leave, and I thanked her with my mind. "Many blessings on your path today, gentlemen," she called over her shoulder as she pedaled down the road.

When she was barely out of earshot, the guys broke out laughing. "Did you see what she was wearing?" Brian said.

"I *know,*" Eddie said. "She needs to crawl into one of those spaceships on her lawn and blast off to Planet Hippie, where she can live among her own kind."

My face got even hotter, but not because I was embarrassed. This time it was because I was starting to get a little mad. Sure, Grandma might dress weird, but I had to admit she'd been pretty nice to me so far. I felt like standing up for her, but I didn't know what to say.

"So, Scrub, is she totally stuck in the sixties like everyone says?" Greg said.

"And is that place half as weird inside as it is outside?" Brian asked.

This was my chance to defend Grandma, but I shrugged and chickened out. "Yeah, I guess," I mumbled. "Look, I gotta go to the store."

"All right," said Eddie. "I *guess* you could still come and play ball with us when you're done. You know, as long as it wouldn't make you miss your flight to Mars." They all laughed, but then Greg punched Eddie in the arm.

"He's just messing around," Greg said to me. "Come find us later. Cool?"

"Okay," I said, but I don't know if they heard. I was sort of talking to my chest. I was pretty mad, but way more at myself for wussing out than at them for making fun of Grandma. I started down the street toward town.

I looked at my watch. Two months, two days, and eighteen hours to go.

6

Leave it to me to get lost in a town as small as Forest Grove. First I passed through the residential part, every lawn perfectly manicured and not a scrap of litter in sight. While I walked through town I was still thinking of lines I should have said to those guys, and I must have missed a turn, because I didn't see a grocery store anywhere. I started to backtrack, when a girl about my age skipped out of a nearby bookstore, swinging a cloth bag. She fell into step right next to me. I only had time to notice that she had long brown hair and a group of freckles spattered across her nose before she started talking; no hello or anything, but talking like we were in the middle of a conversation.

"Did you know the National UFO Reporting Center documents hundreds of sightings every month?" she said.

Huh? I glanced at her, but she was looking straight ahead.

"The National what?" I said. Pretty smooth, I know.

"UFO Reporting Center. It's right here in Washington State."

Oh, there's a group around here that's a little weird? What a surprise.

"Yep, hundreds of reports. Every month," she said. "And that's *after* the center throws out all of the sightings they consider to be hoaxes."

"That's ... um, that's pretty interesting?" I said.

"I'll tell you what's interesting," she said. "First off, it's not like everyone who sees a UFO makes a report. And second, it's not like everyone making reports is seeing the same UFO, right? And third, not every UFO that flies by actually gets seen by somebody." She turned to look at me. Her eyes were so serious that shrugging her off and continuing my walk down the street was not an option. "So you know what that means?"

"No?" I said.

"It means there must be thousands and thousands of UFOs overhead. Tens of thousands. It must be worse than rush hour in Los Angeles up there." She started walking again. With me following, for some reason. "So what's interesting to me about it? I'm surprised there hasn't been a midair collision yet. I mean, doesn't that seem inevitable?"

She was talking like one of the sci-fi/fantasy club types.

Normally I wouldn't be interested in the conversation...but none of those sci-fi/fantasy people was ever a girl who looked this good.

The problem was, I never knew what to say to girls. But Tyler Sandusky was always going off on nonsense arguments like this—one time we debated for a whole weekend about who would win a fight between a man with no arms and a man with no legs—and he expected me to keep up.

So I tried a new tactic with this girl. I said something exactly like I would say it to Tyler. "Well, maybe there are intergalactic traffic laws regulating the buzzing of planets."

The girl smiled. It was sort of a lopsided smile, but it looked nice. It kind of bunched up the freckles across her nose. "Yeah," she said, nodding. "Good point. Like maybe... *Yield the right of way to any UFO traveling over the speed of light.*"

I smiled back. And even thought of something else to say. "Right. Or *Merge with other space vehicles in the same direction that the planet is spinning on its axis.*" Even though we were talking about weird stuff, at least when she laughed, it was with me and not at me.

"Good one," she said. "Very practical. Also *The area above the equator is for multi-passenger UFOs only during peak-flow hours.*"

We reached the edge of town and were heading back into the residential section, and I still hadn't found the store. I stopped at the corner and looked around.

"Looking for something?" the girl asked.

"The grocery store."

"Follow me." She turned and marched down a side street. I jogged a few paces to catch up. She reached into her bag.

"I just bought some good stuff." She held out two books: *Cosmos* and *Alien Agenda: Investigating the Extraterrestrial Presence Among Us*.

Oh, boy. I was surrounded by this kind of thing at Grandma's—was there nowhere in this town to take a break from it? "Why are you so into all that?"

It must have come out a little rude, because she gave me an annoyed look. "I don't know, just kind of a lifelong interest. My dad got me hooked on it when I was little. We watched all kinds of alien movies together."

"Whatever floats your spaceship, I guess."

I smiled and tried to make it sound light, but her forehead creased, and she looked genuinely hurt.

"I thought you'd like these," she said.

"Really? We met five minutes ago."

"Well, aren't you staying at the Intergalactic Bed and Breakfast?"

"How did you know that?"

She shrugged. "Small town."

I looked up and we were there, at the Forest Grove General Store. "Well, thanks for helping me out," I said.

She leaned toward me and dropped her voice a notch. "There's something very interesting going on at that bed-and-breakfast, you know."

"If you say so."

"Did the owner herself send you to the store?"

"Yeah. So?"

"Then I bet you're getting some pretty weird stuff."

"I am not. It's just a normal grocery list." I pulled Grandma's paper out of my pocket.

Tinfoil: 50 boxes
Sunblock SPF 50: 25 bottles
Bleach: As much as you can fit in the cart

Oh no. Not exactly your average trip to the grocery store. I reluctantly looked back at the girl.

Her arms were crossed over her chest and she tilted her head to look at me. "So . . . do you want me to come along and help you find all that 'normal' stuff?"

I glanced at the list. "Um, no thanks. I got it."

"That's what I thought." She raised one eyebrow. "And do you really think you'll be able to find your way back to the bed-and-breakfast all by yourself when you're done?"

"Hmmmm . . . downtown Forest Grove is a pretty huge metropolis, but I think I can manage. A left turn after the third skyscraper, right?"

She laughed. "All right, I'll see you later. My name's Amy, by the way."

"I'm Scrub."

"Nice to meet you, Scrub." She turned, yanked her hair back into a ponytail, then pulled a yellow baseball cap out of her bag and put it on her head. "See ya!" she called, and skipped away. I'm not sure how long I stood in front of the store, mouth hanging open, watching that yellow baseball cap bounce down the road and out of sight—just like yesterday, after she took my picture from the bushes.

I found out what somebody looks like when they're struggling to push a grocery cart overflowing with Reynolds Wrap, Coppertone, and Clorox. They look like a crazy person. At least I did. Especially when the cart got so heavy I lost control as I tried to round a corner. I smashed into a row of shelves and scattered my bottles of suntan lotion all over the floor. When I dropped to my knees to pick them up, someone placed a big black boot in front of my face. I looked up to see the wide face of Sheriff Tate staring at me through his sunglasses, over the rim of his belly. He was chewing on a toothpick so wet and ragged it could've been the same one he had been gnawing when I saw him yesterday.

"Doing a little shopping today, boy?"

I stood and tried to cram the bottles of lotion back into the cart with at least a little dignity, but it was hard to find room. I nodded.

The sheriff studied the mountain of tinfoil spilling out of the grocery cart. "Just picking up the absolute essentials today, huh?"

I shrugged. "Yeah. I guess so."

"My name's Tate. Been the law in this town for over twenty years. This here's Deputy Tisdall." He nodded to a short skinny guy in uniform standing with his back against the candy-bar shelves. His face was tight and pinched, like a rodent. He avoided eye contact and lazily touched one finger to the brim of his hat in greeting.

"And you would be . . . ?"

"My name's Scrub."

"Scrub, huh?" Tate took the toothpick out of his mouth and rolled it around in his fingers. "So, Scrub, I guess you're working at the Space Place now?"

"Um, not really. I mean, I'm staying there. The owner is my grandma."

"Is that right?" he said. Then he just stared at me, but I couldn't see his eyes behind his sunglasses, so it was pretty creepy. "Well, tell me, Scrub, you ever notice anything strange around your grandma's place? Anything weird or unusual?"

About every five minutes. "No," I lied.

The sheriff took another lingering look at the contents of my shopping cart. "Hmmmm, is that right, now?" He stuck the toothpick back in his mouth and used both hands to readjust his belt higher up on Mount Belly. He pulled a business card out of his shirt pocket and thrust it at me. "If you *do* see anything strange, give me a call."

I took the card. "Sure." Another lie. Grandma's place might be weird, but the people there had every right to waste their vacation dollars on that stuff.

We stood there looking at each other. Finally Deputy Tisdall said, "I guess you better start hauling that cart full of goodies back to your grandma's. We wouldn't want her esteemed *guests* to go without their precious supplies, would we?"

I pushed past them, steering the cart toward the cashier. I could feel their stares crawling all over my back until I walked out the front door. I was sure glad to get out of there, but when I stepped into the sunshine, my stomach was suddenly full of dread. I didn't want to run into those teenagers again while I was hauling this weird cargo around. And as much as I hated to admit it, Tate and his deputy had raised an interesting point. I had no idea what Grandma and her customers *were* going to do with all of this stuff. And I really didn't want to find out.

7

When I finally made it back to Grandma's, drenched in sweat, I realized there was no possible way I could drag the grocery cart up the stairs to the front porch. I slumped against the cart, panting, and dried my forehead on my sleeve.

Mr. Harnox walked out the door and down the steps, that ghastly smile stretched across his entire face. "Oh, so many thanks and thanks again for the little man," he said, and sniffed the grocery cart all over. Then he grabbed a box of Reynolds Wrap. Before I could answer, he pulled out the roll of aluminum foil, tore off a huge chunk, wadded it into a ball, and crammed it into his mouth.

He smacked loudly, silver-colored drool trickling down his cheeks. Little sparks shot out of his mouth as those sharp teeth hit the foil. He threw his head back to look at the sky while he swallowed, shaking his throat and bobbing his head like a pelican choking down a big fish.

Then he withdrew a thin metal tube from the pocket inside his vest, punctured the side of a tub of bleach, and started sucking on the thing like a juice box. I just stared. He set the Clorox down and was tearing off another chunk of foil when Grandma appeared on the porch.

She raced down the steps, scanning the street warily. She placed her hand on the tall man's arm. "Let's take your snacks and go into the house, shall we?"

Mr. Harnox grinned. He wrapped his long arms around the entire grocery cart, hoisted it into the air as if it weighed nothing, and bounded up the steps. He slipped into the house, angling sideways to fit the cart through the door.

I looked after the tall gray man in disbelief. Grandma studied my face. "The time has arrived for you and me to have a talk, Scrub."

"Can we start with why that guy is chowing down on tinfoil?"

Grandma put her arm around me and led me up the steps. "Yes, that does look a bit unpleasant, doesn't it? But I guess it helps. Apparently the aluminum oxide slows down the corrosive effect of Earth's atmosphere on poor Mr. Harnox's body. It helps him enjoy his time here, but he needs to eat quite a bit of it every day." We reached the door, and Grandma glanced back to check the street again. "And the bleach. I can't tell if that's to clean out his system, or if he just likes the taste." She sighed. "It has put a strain on the grocery bill. After two years he's eating me out of house and home with the tinfoil bill alone."

Right...

I looked at Grandma. She wasn't kidding.

We walked into the front room and sat on the couch. We were alone, but I could hear Mr. Harnox chomping and slurping away behind the kitchen door.

"Scrub, did your father tell you why he sent you here this summer?"

Good question. For the last couple of weeks, whenever I asked him the same thing, he had tried to change the subject or said that he had work to do. I figured that Grandma's place was a last-resort destination when those summer business trips popped up for him and Mom. I thought that maybe he just didn't want to argue with me about it.

But when he'd pulled the car up to the curb under the big departures sign at the airport yesterday, he had started talking real fast. Said that my seeing where he grew up might help the two of us get closer, and he'd always wanted that. Told me that I was growing up so fast, and there were some things I had to learn on my own. Claimed that if I paid attention, my experiences this summer could change my life.

At the time, I had thought it was just parent-speak. I mean, that had all seemed like a lot to ask for a couple of months at a weird little rustic inn. But Dad doesn't really ever talk about touchy-feely stuff, so I knew enough to keep my mouth shut. Not that there was time for a Q&A session anyway. Dad had just kind of looked through the windshield during his little speech; then when it was over, he'd hopped out of the car and helped me grab my suitcase, and a few minutes later I was getting in line at security and saying good-bye.

I looked up at Grandma. I didn't really know how to say all of that to her, so I just shrugged.

She reached out and patted my hand. "He didn't give me the clearest instructions, either." She winked at me. "My only child has many fine talents, but I'm afraid that having conversations of a personal nature is not one of them."

I snorted. That was an understatement. Then I noticed how uncomfortable I was having this conversation with Grandma and realized that I was probably just like him.

Grandma smoothed out her tunic on her lap. "But I suppose the fact that he sent you here alone, for the whole summer, gives me at least tacit permission to share a few things with you."

I glanced at the kitchen door. I was having a hard time figuring out the role that Mr. Harnox and his strange eating habits were supposed to play in this little family drama.

"For starters, I believe in serendipity, Scrub, well and truly, and your arrival has been very serendipitous indeed."

"Oh. Yeah?" I said. I didn't really know what that word meant.

"Yes. First and foremost, I've always wanted the chance to get to know my only grandchild." She reached over to the table beside the couch, picked up a picture of my dad when he was a kid, and sighed. "The wheel of the cosmos spins and spins, and the best we can do is hope to hold on," she said, studying the old photo. She was quiet for a while, then she brushed away a tear at the corner of one eye. "It was just me and your father when he was growing up here. I'm afraid that I made some mistakes, and I don't want to make them twice." She placed the picture back on the table and looked at me again.

"But there is another reason I am so thankful for your arrival, Scrub. A very important reason." She was really studying me through those big pink lenses, looking me right in the eye. "You see, I have come to require more and more help around here. But it's impossible for me to just hire anyone from around town." She put her hand on top of mine. "I needed to be able to observe how someone from the outside would interact with my guests. And you've acted very natural and friendly with everyone since you arrived. You've been very helpful already, even in such a short amount of time. Something tells me you would be a fine ambassador for us."

"Ambassador? For *us*? Us who?"

Grandma spread her arms out. "Our species. Here on Earth. Humanity."

Oh, no. I knew right where this was headed. I could see it perfectly: an intergalactic picnic in the backyard, with each of the guests dressed up as their favorite alien, and me playing the part of welcoming leader of the human race. I'm sure she had a costume for that around here somewhere. Is that the kind of stuff she had done with Dad when he was a kid? Is that why he irons his bathrobe and wears pleated slacks around the house on weekends—a desperate attempt to be normal after such a strange childhood?

Well, Grandma would have to see if the costume fit Amy, that UFO-obsessed girl I met in town, because there was no way I was putting it on.

I opened my mouth to say this when Grandma put up her hand to stop me. Then she dropped her hands to her lap and fidgeted with them. She took a deep breath. "I was going to wait a week or two to decide whether we would have this talk, Scrub. But everything has been so busy lately." She looked up at me and smiled. "And you've done so well thus far. Plus, I've always trusted my intuition. And I can tell you will do a great job just by seeing your aura. Your aura glows almost turquoise with your positivity and good nature."

Right. I didn't really know what the word *aura* meant, either, but I wasn't about to ask.

We looked at each other for a moment. I tried to steer her toward some of the more normal things that I might be able to do this summer. "So...you want me to help you out around here?" I said. "Like going to the store this morning? Or mowing the lawn or whatever? Because I could do that stuff if you want."

"Well, yes, I have more and more errands that need doing. But it's more than that." She put both hands on my shoulders. "My instincts tell me that I can trust you. Can I truly trust you, Scrub?"

"Of course." She was acting like the sole keeper of a national defense secret. But what secret could be that important when you ran a tourist trap in the middle of nowhere?

"How to start?" she said, glancing at the ceiling as if maybe the answer were printed there. "It all began when

I got a visit from the most wonderful...no, that's not the best way to begin." She smoothed her hair down and bit her lower lip. "Well, it just so happened that...No. No, that's not right either." She stood, walked to the bookshelf, and grabbed something. "Here, it might be easiest if you read this."

She handed me a thin brochure. The cover read *Your Vacation on Earth*. I looked up at Grandma with my eyebrows wrinkled. "Just give it a chance," she said.

I opened the pamphlet. Instantly, several holographic images appeared, floating right in front of my face, about a foot above the brochure. My whole body flinched, and I snapped the brochure closed. The holograms disappeared.

Grandma patted my hand. "All is well," she said.

I eased open the brochure again, and the images leaped into the air. A blue-green globe of Earth, about a foot in diameter, spun slowly on its axis in front of my eyes. It looked so real. The colors were bright and it was one of those globes where the mountains stick up and everything. Holding the brochure in one hand, I tried to touch the globe, but my hand slipped right through the image. "Wait a moment," Grandma said. Pretty soon a red arrow appeared and pointed to the northwestern part of the United States with the words *You are here!* flashing next to it.

Beside this was a floating three-dimensional image of an overweight couple on a cruise ship, in brightly colored Hawaiian shirts and matching visors, with enough cameras and video equipment draped around their necks to drown them if they fell off the ship. The guy was even wearing dark socks pulled up to his bone-white knees.

The people waved. A floating caption underneath read, *Two earthlings set out for a day of vacation.* The following words scrolled by underneath the image like the headline ticker on those twenty-four-hour news channels:

STEP BACK IN TIME WITH A VISIT TO THIS QUAINT LITTLE PLANET HIDDEN AWAY IN A QUIET CORNER OF THE MILKY WAY GALAXY. EARTH IS THE ONLY INHABITED PLANET IN ITS TINY SOLAR SYSTEM, MAKING IT THE PERFECT RELAXING GETAWAY. THE TRANSPORTER RECEPTION AREA—LOCATED AT AN ESTABLISHMENT KNOWN LOCALLY AS THE INTERGALACTIC BED AND BREAKFAST—IS IN AN AREA LARGELY UNTOUCHED BY EARTHLING "CIVILIZATION." THIS ALLOWS TRAVELERS TO ENJOY EARTH IN ITS NATURAL STATE WITH EASY ACCESS TO THIS PLANET'S ABUNDANT PLANT AND ANIMAL LIFE.

I stared at the holographs. I was about to say something like "This can't be real" or "I don't believe this"... but then I heard the gray dude in the kitchen, chomping and smacking his way through who knew how many rolls of aluminum foil. My fingers remembered touching that squishy, so-moist-it-was-almost-slimy hand, and I shuddered.

I leaned my head toward the kitchen door and whispered, "So... Mr. Harnox is... you know... an *alien*... really?"

Grandma nodded. "He's visiting from the planet Shuunuu in the Andromeda galaxy," she said. "Poor thing. He was only supposed to stay the weekend, but complications forced him into a rather extended visit."

My mind went numb. If Mr. Harnox was really an... then

that might mean they *all* were: the family on all fours . . . the kid with the lumpy head . . . and the people sleeping *right next door* to me all night long, and—

Grandma pulled me out of my thoughts. "Oh, and I don't care much for the word *alien*. It sounds harsh." She glanced at the kitchen door, then back at me. "It comes with such a negative connotation and denotes the 'other.' I try to focus on our similarities. I prefer the term *Tourist*, if you don't mind."

I nodded, as if I somehow understood. My mouth had gone totally dry. "So this brochure, who sees it?"

"Those are distributed at vacation centers throughout every galaxy in the cosmos," Grandma said.

I took another long look at the tacky tourists, waving and smiling at me. "So the entire universe thinks we all look like dorks?" I said.

My mind flooded with a million questions. I picked one at random. "So how do the aliens—I mean the *Tourists*—get here? Do spaceships land in the backyard?"

Grandma laughed. "Oh, no. That's an Earth myth about space travel. UFO sightings and crop circles and all the rest." She took the brochure and put it back on the bookshelf. "Spaceships are used almost exclusively for trade cargo these days, transporting bulky goods from planet to planet. And for interstellar law enforcement, I suppose. But strictly business. When aliens travel for recreation, they use the transporter system pretty much exclusively."

My mind buzzed. Grandma's place doesn't get cell phone service or the Internet, but she knows the secret to space travel?

"Transporters?"

"Yes. Each room here has one."

I nodded. The closet door with the glowing blue circle. I didn't realize how lucky I was when that thing wouldn't open in the middle of the night. Where would I have ended up if I'd stumbled in there? I was going to have to be very careful around this place. "How do they work?"

"Well, it's a bit complicated, and I don't fully understand it myself. But basically a Tourist steps into a transporter on his home planet. He is scanned, then broken down into his most basic elements."

"Elements? Like the periodic table?"

"Exactly. The elements are the same all over the universe. We are all of us—humans and space Tourists alike—made up of the exact same stuff. I have always thought that to be the most wonderful notion. It fills me with such hope." Grandma looked sort of dreamy and far away again.

"So . . . the Tourists are broken down into elements. . . ." I said, hoping to get her back on track.

"That's right. The elements are dissipated across the Tourist's home planet. The scan is sent to our machines, and the same elements are drawn from our atmosphere and assembled to create the original being. The genetic information remains intact, and you get the same creature that shows up here, nearly instantaneously, even though the Tourist might live millions of light-years away."

Yikes. "Does it hurt?" I said.

"Oh, no. Just a tickle. At least that's what the Tourists tell me. Apparently it all happens instantaneously. Before you're even fully broken down in one place, you're being put back together in another."

I thought of my room again. "That thing—the transporter—it went off in my room in the middle of the night." I shuddered again. "Could something just pop out of there?" If so, I wasn't going to be able to fall asleep for the next two months.

Grandma shook her head and patted me on the hand. "That one's been on the fritz for years. It sparkles on and off every now and again, but no Tourists can use it. I've tried to get it fixed, but it's so hard to get a repairman to visit a primitive planet. A couple of the others have been short-circuiting on me, but no one from the Interstellar Tourism Bureau can be bothered."

Mr. Harnox walked through the kitchen door and smiled at us as he passed by. I gawked as he went up the stairs, his lanky legs taking them five at a time.

"His planet had a bit of an immigration problem," Grandma whispered. "The government there completely overreacted and shut down the transporter system right after Mr. Harnox arrived here. He's been stuck ever since."

Poor dude. The questions kept coming. "Aren't you worried about calling this place the *Intergalactic* Bed and Breakfast? With the space decorations and all? Aren't you afraid someone will find out?"

Grandma smiled. "We're hiding out in the open. Do you think anyone would believe me if I told them that actual aliens visited here?"

Good point. Unless you count Amy, I guess, but I had a feeling she'd be willing to believe anything you told her about aliens. "Well, what about your human customers?"

"Human customers?" Grandma said. "I haven't had a human customer since..." She squinted and looked up. "I don't think I've *ever* had a human customer."

Wow. I was trying to soak it all in when the most obvious question of all occurred to me. "Does Dad know?"

Grandma took a deep breath. "I opened the inn when he was a baby, it's true," she said. "But things were different back then, when he was growing up. We didn't have a brochure put together yet or even a blurb in the Interstellar Tourism Bureau guide, so business was very slow. We got the occasional honeymooners looking for an ultra-secluded getaway spot, but folks like that always spent most of the time in their room."

Ugh. Thanks for that mental image, Grandma. I don't want to picture aliens making more aliens. I must have made a face, because she looked at me and laughed a little bit before she continued. "And we had a few xenoscientists and planetary researchers, but they were always outside, taking pictures and collecting soil and water samples." Grandma shrugged. "There was much that I was able to hide from him."

She gazed out the window with a look on her face like she was seeing things that happened a long time ago. She sighed. "Poor little guy. His mother was the town kook, after all, and he wanted so badly to fit in. He threw himself into school, clubs, student government, sports. Created his own world, his own sense of reality. Worked on projects at school until all hours, stayed over with friends, but never brought them here. The older he got, the less we saw of each other."

I was having trouble picturing Dad as a kid. It was easy to believe that he'd started life as a six-footer in a sports jacket with a cell phone attached to his ear.

Grandma shifted uncomfortably in her seat. "Once he reached his teen years, certain things became obvious. But still I kept a few secrets. And then, before we took the chance to talk about everything, he was off to the University of Florida. It was the farthest away that he could go and still be in the same country." She was quiet for a long time, then finally said, "I think you should to talk to your father if you have any more questions about his experiences here."

I just sat there thinking about the fact that I was in on a secret that maybe only two other people in the world knew. My heart sped up. I wasn't sure I was ready. The C-minus I'd gotten in science didn't exactly qualify me to be humanity's ambassador to visitors from the depths of space.

Grandma lifted her gaze from the floor, tears making her eyes shiny behind those pink lenses. "You look so much like him, Scrub, when he was your age. It feels like a chance for me to start over. I hope that makes some sort of sense."

I sat up a little straighter and nodded. Nobody had ever trusted me like this before. I didn't want to let her down. I had so many more questions, but before I could open my mouth—

Ding! Ding! Ding!

A series of chimes came from the cupboard with the keys. "Follow me, Scrub." Down the hallway, Grandma opened the cupboard. Next to the key for room 3B, a little green light flashed in time with the chimes.

"Well, it looks like we'll be able to give you some on-the-job training. One of the things I desperately need help with is GRADEs."

"Grades?"

"Greeting and Review of Alien's Disguise for Earth. A most important process." Grandma opened a side door to a supply closet. She spoke to me over her shoulder as she rummaged around. "It's essential that no one discovers our secret here, of course. You know how people treat those who are different. You can imagine what folks would do if they knew visitors from outer space were here."

I had seen enough movies to get a clear picture. Guns, tanks, missiles. Secret experiments in underground labs.

Grandma stepped out of the closet and handed me a suitcase. A placard on the front read COMPLETE STAGE MAKEUP AND ACCESSORIES KIT. "But nosy humans are the least of my concerns, to tell you the truth. What's worse is that if my secret is discovered, the folks at the Interstellar Tourism Bureau will take away my hotelier license. Probably permanently."

"Really?"

"Oh, yes. The bureau is already touchy about granting licenses to hoteliers on primitive planets, but I had a friend pull a few strings for me. It probably wouldn't take much for them to revoke my license. I try to maintain a very low profile."

I sat on the couch and set the suitcase across my knees. Inside was everything you might need for making disguises:

face paint, fake noses, mustaches, that sort of thing. "What do you do with all of this stuff?"

"When Tourists arrive, we need to make sure they are ready to mingle with the people of Earth."

"So we use this stuff to make sure they look...normal?"

Grandma sniffed. "'Normal' as it's narrowly defined on Earth, anyway. Many of them have done their research and have already disguised themselves the best they can to fit in. But my heavens, some of the others think any old carbon-based life form can just drop in here and walk around unnoticed." She shook her head. "They're used to vacationing on planets where the citizens are more accustomed to off-world guests, I suppose." She turned and walked up the first few stairs. "Bring the kit and follow me, Scrub. Those folks should be arriving in Three-B any time now."

I followed Grandma up the steps. We were almost at the second-floor landing when someone knocked on the front door. Grandma glanced at her watch. "Oh, dear. That's probably UPS with the weekly delivery. You see what I mean? Not enough time for one woman to do it all. Lately, it seems like GRADE jobs alone have been taking up most of my time." She started back down the steps. "Do you think you could hold down the fort up in Three-B for a minute? Just until I can make my way up there?"

Me? Like, by myself, me?

"Is this...I mean, do you think...is all of this safe?"

"In forty years, I've never had a problem with a Tourist." She waved me up the stairs. "Just make some small talk. Stall them until I can get up there and walk you through a full GRADE session." Grandma headed down the stairs again, then turned when she reached the bottom. "See if they speak enough English to get by. That can be pretty hit-and-miss, I'm afraid." Then she was around the corner and out of sight.

I swallowed. Maybe it's easy for her to handle the sudden arrival of space aliens, but my heart pounded as I trudged up the steps. Sure, there are movies where aliens are friendly and want to help people, like *E.T.* or *Superman*. But I've seen way more movies where the aliens want to suck human brains out of their ear holes or hatch eggs inside their bodies. It took all my willpower to put one foot in front of the other and lug myself to the third floor.

9

By the time I made it up the second staircase to room 3B, I could feel cold beads of sweat on my forehead, and damp patches under my armpits. I knocked, but no answer. The door creaked as I eased it open.

I sat on the bed and waited, breathing deeply to calm down my heart rate.

A glowing blue circle appeared in the center of the "closet" door, pulsing faster and faster until it became a constant bright blue. That thrumming sound matched the pulsing lights until it turned into a steady whine.

I stood and took a couple of steps toward the door. This was crazy. And probably dangerous. I could not do this. I hadn't done anything this dangerous since the last time Tyler challenged me to—

That's it! The Challenges. Just think of this as one of the Challenges. Pretend Tyler's Colossal Summer Challenge was Meet An Alien. No Wussing Out.

It probably sounds stupid, but this helped. My heart calmed down, and I was able to catch my breath. I've done all kinds of scary things because I *had* to, because there's no backing down from a Challenge. I waited for the arrival.

The thrumming whine from the blue circle hit its highest note, then stopped suddenly. A cloud of steam seeped from underneath the door and curled toward the ceiling. There was a faint *whoosh* sound. The door slowly opened.

The steam cleared, and standing before me were two aliens.

They must have studied that brochure, because they matched the tacky tourists almost exactly, with too-bright Hawaiian shirts and visors and everything.

"Hel-lo," said the male (or what I assumed was the male). "You are first Earth creature we are meeting." He took a quick glance at a book-shaped device in his hand, stuck his arm straight out, and said, "Would you enjoy to hold my hand and shake it up and down in the gesture of greeting?"

"Okay." I shook his hand. It was really cold. And I don't mean clammy, but freezing to the touch.

"That was great!" he said.

"Thanks . . . I've done it before."

"Of course. You live here!" He barked out a series of

high-pitched squeals. A big smile stretched his face, so I guessed he was laughing.

I tried to smile back. The three of us stared at each other for a minute. The male certainly seemed friendly, but I wasn't sure about the female. She had only been here two minutes and already she had the Earth-sneer down perfectly. I strained my hearing, praying for the sound of Grandma's footsteps coming down the hall. If you told me a week ago I would meet a space alien, I'm sure I could've come up with a thousand good questions for it. But I was a total blank now.

I kept staring. In an attempt to make this appear less rude, I started nodding. No idea why, except maybe it would seem reassuring, or at least nonthreatening. The male must've thought it was another Earth ritual, like shaking hands, so he copied me. And then it was like I didn't know how to stop. So we just stood there, bobbing our heads at one another like a couple of mental patients.

The female looked annoyed. "Can we make the exit soon? Now?"

That pulled me out of it. I stopped nodding. "Uh...actually, you need to wait here for a bit."

"For what reason?" she said.

"You need to be...ah...GRADEd."

"What?"

"Well, your Earth disguises...they need to be reviewed or inspected or whatever, and then—"

"Inspected?" She spat the word.

"To make sure, you know, you're ready. Ready to go out. Outside."

She sighed heavily. "Hurry and be finished, then."

"Actually, I'm not the one who—"

"We paid real money for this little vacation. Get started," she said.

I looked at the door, silently willing Grandma to appear. Nothing. The female tapped her foot on the floor in what must be the universal signal of impatience.

I'd better at least try to get started. Grandma wanted them to look "normal," so I checked them out. They looked fine, overall...but with a closer look I noticed something that might count as out of the ordinary.

"Sir? You have sort of a bright purple patch on your cheek."

"So sorry. You are the expert, yes? You can help?"

Expert. Right. At least he couldn't tell I had only been on the job for five minutes.

I shifted my weight from one foot to the other, looking back and forth between the aliens. They stared back at me. I nodded at them some more and cleared my throat, trying to fill the awkward silence. Maybe Grandma shouldn't have trusted me so much after all.

"Well, what are you thinking to do about this?" the female said.

I noticed a box of Kleenex on the bedside table. In desperation, I grabbed a couple of tissues and approached the male. He bent down and offered me his cheek.

I rubbed at the purple spot. Bad idea. The purple patch grew. It was freezing, just like his hands, and sort of...scaly. I panicked, and rubbed harder. Rubbery, flesh-colored chunks fell from his face as the Kleenex scraped away the disguise to reveal his true skin. Another chunk fell away, and a third eye, set in the middle of his cheekbone, opened up and stared at me. I shuddered. Part of his lip had rubbed off, and a few sharp fangs poked out the side of his face.

I managed to stop my frantic rubbing and step back. I had turned a mostly normal-looking Tourist into an extra from a flesh-eating-zombie movie.

"I don't know overly much about this little planet around here, but I don't think you're helping," the female said.

"Nonsense, let the man do his duties," the male said. He gave me a smile that was probably meant to be friendly but looked pretty gruesome, given his circumstances.

I was lost. Little beads of cold sweat popped out on my forehead. I put my hands behind my back so the aliens wouldn't see them shaking.

Finally, Grandma glided into the room, a huge smile on her face. "Welcome to Earth, travelers," she said, spreading her arms wide. "We are so happy you could visit with us today." She gave each alien a big hug, then stepped back and put her arm around me. "I see you've met Scrub. He's my grandson and new employee." She looked at me. "How is everything going?"

"Oh, you know, fine," I lied. "They just, um, I mean we need to maybe fix him up a little bit. Right around that region." I pointed to the male alien's face.

"Of course, no problem at all," Grandma said. She was very calm, just like everything was perfectly normal. I realized that to her, at least, this was probably true.

She popped open the stage makeup kit and pulled out a vial of flesh-colored liquid. "I find this to be the best for cover-up work," Grandma told me. She stepped in front of the male alien. "Close that lower eye, please. Thank you." She tipped the vial upside down onto a tiny sponge, then rubbed the makeup over the alien's third eye. It disappeared with a couple of circular swipes.

Grandma turned and handed me the sponge. "Here, Scrub. Do you think you could finish with the cheek while I touch up that lip?"

"Um, sure." I stepped in beside Grandma and dabbed at the alien's face. It took me a lot longer than her to get the makeup spread evenly, but eventually those purple scales faded.

Grandma reached inside the kit and pulled out a thin sheet of flesh-colored rubber. "Prosthetic skin," she said to me. She cut a couple of strips using tiny scissors, then opened a short bottle. The cap had a little brush sticking out of the middle that dipped into the bottle when it was closed, which she touched to the rubber skin. "This is spirit gum," she told me. "Very sticky, and long-lasting. Stage actors use it to attach false mustaches or a patch of scar tissue."

I continued rubbing makeup on the alien's face. Grandma nestled in next to us and pressed the rubber skin against his lips, re-forming the bits I had rubbed off. Then she dabbed at the new lips with some pink-colored paints. We finished up at the same time.

We stepped back for a look. Amazing. It had taken Grandma less than two minutes to clean up my hideous mess.

"Now, how do we look?" the male alien said. He spread his arms to present himself, and a third arm popped out from the middle of his shirt where one of the buttons had come undone. It was also purple and scaly. That would probably count as out of the ordinary for Forest Grove.

I waited for Grandma to answer, but she just looked at me, one eyebrow raised. "You, um, probably want to keep *that* out of sight," I said, gesturing vaguely toward the arm sticking out of his chest. Grandma winked at me and nodded.

"Oh, yes, right you are," he said, and the arm slithered back into the shirt. "Now I am remembering. Your people just have the two of them. But I am not being certain of how you manage with just two!" He let loose with that barking laugh again.

"Is that all?" the lady alien asked. Grandma had to help with her hair—her curly gray wig was a little lopsided—but otherwise she looked fine.

"You two look adorable. You're all ready for a vacation," Grandma said. "Let me give you some maps of the area. There are excellent hiking trails if you would like to explore the natural aspects of Earth. Follow me downstairs, and I can give you a full orientation on how to behave among Earthlings before you head out."

Grandma held the door open and motioned for them to exit. As the male alien was walking toward the door, he held out his hand to me. I moved to shake his hand again, but instead he dropped a half dozen tiny cubes into my outstretched palm. They were a shiny metallic green, and when I touched them, neon colors flashed all over their sides.

"What are these?" I said.

"What's the matter? Not enough for you?" the female alien said.

"Oh, no, that's a most generous tip," Grandma said. "I'm sure Scrub is quite grateful."

I stared at the little flashing cubes, then up at the male

alien. "Thanks," I said. I didn't bother to add, *I'm sure this money will come in handy. You know, the next time I visit your planet.*

Grandma ushered the aliens out the door. When they were in the hall, she turned and whispered, "Wonderful job, Scrub. I'm so proud."

"But you did everything," I said.

"You kept your cool, that's the most important thing," Grandma said. "You should have seen me at first. I was so nervous I let my first customer walk right out the front door with bright yellow tentacles sticking out the armholes of his shirt. I chased him down the street and hauled him back here after I realized. Trust me, you were terrific."

"Thanks." My face got a little hot. I wasn't really used to doing any important jobs back home.

I looked down at my hands and remembered the chill of the alien's bare skin against mine. I couldn't help but shiver a little bit. "Those Tourists seemed pretty nice, but still... are you totally sure it's all safe? I don't mean that I thought they were going to attack me or anything. But is it, like, *environmentally* safe? I don't know, with them bringing in alien germs or whatever?"

"I've been doing this almost forty years, and I've never caught a Venusian virus or gotten so much as the sniffles from a Saturnian sickness. It's safe, all right." She grinned at me. "Besides, I've seen some of the places that young boys put their hands right here on germ-filled Earth. A few dust particles from a distant planet should be the least of your worries." I blushed at that, even though I wasn't quite sure why. "But I can buy a couple of bottles of hand sanitizer to have around the house if it makes you feel better."

I shrugged. "It's okay. I trust you."

Grandma moved closer and cupped my face in her hands. "I feel I can really trust you, as well. Now, in all seriousness, our most important job is to make sure that no one finds out the truth about our guests. I sincerely hope there is a time when Earth can handle this knowledge, but I'm afraid that time is not now."

I nodded, and my face got even warmer. "I promise to keep your secret."

"It's such a blessing to have you here, Scrub." Grandma leaned in and kissed my forehead. "I'm glad we got some training in. While I was downstairs, the sensors went off to indicate three more arrivals on this floor. I think you are going to be very busy today!"

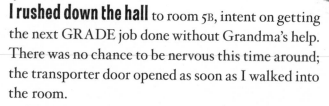

10

I rushed down the hall to room 5B, intent on getting the next GRADE job done without Grandma's help. There was no chance to be nervous this time around; the transporter door opened as soon as I walked into the room.

The thing that crawled out of the transporter looked like a squid. It was about half as tall as me, but most of that height consisted of its enormous round head, which was purplish red with green swirls and covered on all sides with tiny blinking eyes. Maybe a hundred of them. It slithered along the floor with the help of at least a dozen snakelike arms, covered in tentacles, which sprang straight out of its neck.

I looked down at the stage kit in my hands. Somehow I didn't think a touch of makeup and a fake mustache were going to enable this particular Tourist to blend in with the citizens of Forest Grove.

Suddenly all of the creature's eyes slammed shut, except for four or five that looked directly at me. Then he started shouting.

"ϧႅϵχϡҜШЧЖ♪‡║╟!!!"

What the...? I may not have understood the words, but even someone with only half an hour of training in greeting aliens could tell he was upset.

"I'm sorry, um... sir? I can't tell what you're saying."

The alien stuck the tip of one of those snake arms into a hole in his head—an ear?—and twirled it around. Then he withdrew it with a sucking sound and tapped the side of his head a few times.

"What kind of reception chamber is this for an ocean planet?" he suddenly spluttered. "This is unacceptable!"

Gumball-size gobs of purple slime flew out of his mouth as he spoke, and splattered all over the front of my T-shirt. They smelled like low tide.

"Well... um... I'm not exactly sure that I—"

"What are you, some kind of snarffle-eating tumblerite? I must speak with management at once!" He was getting really loud. "Tell me that there is something approaching intelligent life on this planet. I demand that—"

"What seems to be the problem here?" Grandma asked as she glided into the room. I was half embarrassed and half relieved that she was here to bail me out again. "Oh, dear, it looks like someone must have been sent to the wrong vacation destination."

"I should say so! I'm supposed to be arriving on the ocean planet of Krustacia. Where have I been transported to?"

"You're on Earth, I'm afraid," Grandma said.

"Earth? Never heard of it," he scoffed.

I tried to think of something I could do to help Grandma, but my mind was blank. "Take heart, friend," she said. "We can get you right back into the transporter and safely home in no time at all."

"Oh, no you don't," the squid-thing shouted, his tentacled limbs working furiously as he slithered away from me and Grandma and backed into a corner. "I'm not transporting home yet. I have paid my money in the full and proper amount and I *will* be taking my rightful vacation."

Grandma took me by the arm and pulled me toward the door. "No problem, sir," she said as we headed out of the room. "We'll get everything fixed right away for you. Just wait here for a moment."

She whispered as she led me down the hallway. "More troubles with the transporters. I do wish I could get someone here to look at that one." She unlocked a storage closet at the end of the hall and rummaged through it. "We need to get that Tourist in some water quickly. If memory serves, his kind is from the planet Mussatonia, and if he's dry too much longer he's liable to shrivel up and die."

"That's horrible," I said.

"I know. You can smell a dead Mussatonian for miles around! I'd never be able to get that odor out of the carpet."

Grandma gave me a wry smile. She might be old, but I respected how calm she was during this tense moment. I realized that, in a weird way, I could learn something from watching her; a good point guard needed the same kind of poise under pressure. I breathed deep and tried to get my jittery feeling to go away.

I pushed some boxes out of Grandma's way as she moved toward the back corner of the closet. She searched quietly for a few moments, which allowed me to gather my thoughts.

"That Tourist's English seems really good," I said.

"Oh, I suspect he's cheating," Grandma said. She glanced up from looking through boxes, saw the confused look on my face, and continued. "He probably has a translator—a tiny computer crystal lodged in his brain that turns his thoughts into words we can understand. Lots of Tourists use them. Technically, that type of sophisticated technology is not supposed to be used on primitive planets, but I usually let it slide. Makes my job easier, to be honest."

Whoa. Alien technology sounded pretty cool. "Could humans build something like that?" I said. Intro to Spanish homework would be a lot easier. "How do they work?"

She shrugged. "Honestly, I have no idea."

"Really? Aren't you curious?"

Grandma stopped rummaging for a moment and smiled at me. "If you went to another planet, could you tell them how a TV set really works? In enough detail so they could build one of their own? Or do you just accept the fact that it works somehow and watch TV shows?"

I grinned sheepishly. "Good point."

Grandma went back to her search. "Ah, here we are!" She

moved some blankets and uncovered a huge aquarium. "Perfect. I know it's only your first day on the job, but we're going to add Chaperone to your official title."

Eeesh. I wasn't sure I liked the sound of that. "Chaperone?"

I helped Grandma push the aquarium—it was too heavy to carry—down the hall to the bathroom, where she started filling it up with water. "Yes. If we don't give that Tourist some kind of vacation experience, he's likely to fill out a negative comment form and send it to the Interstellar Tourism Bureau." Grandma winked. "And I don't want to soil my perfect forty-year record of service. So if you could just run him down to the river, let him splash around a little bit, I'm sure he'll be fine."

"Ummmm . . . are you sure that's a good idea? Taking him outside?"

"Oh, the river trail is only a few hundred yards away. You shouldn't see anyone. But if you do, just tell them he's your pet squid or something."

I was starting to think that maybe Grandma was getting a little too comfortable with the aliens after hanging around them for forty years.

But fifteen minutes later I was pulling a bright red Radio Flyer wagon down the front walkway. Perched on top of the wagon was the aquarium, half filled with water, with Mr. Squid-Man packed into it. It was a pretty tight fit, and a good part of his head stuck up and over the rim. The whole contraption weighed about a thousand pounds, but Mr. Harnox had carried it down the stairs for me, no problem.

When we reached the front gate, one of Mr. Squid-Man's arms snaked over a glass side to swat at the swarm of mosquitoes buzzing around his head. A woman—a *human* woman—was running down the road, pushing a toddler in a jogging stroller. The toddler pointed at the aquarium and laughed. The woman gave us a strange look and crossed to the other side of the street.

"Stop that!" I hissed. Now that I was actually outside with one of the aliens, I couldn't stop thinking about the promise I had made to Grandma: I would do anything I could to help keep her secret.

The wheels on the wagon squeaked as I pulled it down the walkway. "This is an outrage!" Mr. Squid-Man said. "I have never heard tell of such a degrading form of transportation!"

"And no talking, either. You promised." I had to grab that slimy arm and sort of stuff it back into the aquarium.

When he was finally still, I opened the gate and dragged the wagon through. It was really heavy. I was able to move it pretty steadily on the asphalt, but when I turned onto the trail by the park, a little dirt path that led down to the Nooksack River, I had to heave on it just to get it to roll a few feet before it lurched to a stop. Then I'd have to rest a moment before I gave another two-armed pull.

So when I saw some people walking over from the park, there was no possible way to run and hide.

"Hey, it's Scrub the Space Boy!" Eddie called out as the three teens neared. Oh, no. I realized I hadn't seen these guys since I bailed on them after promising to meet up and play ball at the park, and this was not the best time for a second meeting.

"Whatcha doin'?"

"Oh, nothing. You know. Just taking a walk." What else

could I say? I tried not to acknowledge the presence of the little kid's wagon and the aquarium and the purple alien.

"What's that?" Greg asked, pointing at the little kid's wagon and the aquarium and the purple alien.

"Oh, you know." I swallowed. "Just...a squid. He's my pet." I heard Mr. Squid-Man scoff at that, so I sort of nudged him in the head with my elbow to remind him of our agreement on silence.

"You have a pet *squid*?" Brian said. "And you take him for walks?" They all started cracking up. I sort of looked at the ground. "Let me guess, that was your grandma's idea."

Eddie had grabbed a fallen branch and was sneaking up behind Mr. Squid-Man, reaching out like maybe he was going to poke the alien. That would be a disaster. I had to—

"Oh, leave him alone, you guys." My head jerked up at the new voice, and I saw Amy stepping out from behind some trees. "You just don't know anything because you've never been out of Forest Grove in your whole life. I bet lots of people in Florida have squids for pets. Right, Scrub?"

"Ummmm, right," I said. It wasn't remotely true, of course, but I was grateful that she was sticking up for me.

The three teens looked at each other and then took a couple of steps backward, away from Amy. Eddie dropped his stick onto the dirt path. "Well, all right, Space Boy," Brian said. "If your pet squid ever learns how to play fetch or catch a Frisbee, then maybe you can hang out with us at the park." They turned and walked away, still laughing.

I turned back to look at Amy. "Thanks."

"No problem."

"You know, they almost seemed afraid of you."

"They know who not to mess with." Amy shrugged. "Usually they're not too bad. They just like to make fun of things they don't understand." She rolled her eyes. "Unfortunately, that seems to include almost everything."

"Right..." I just sort of stood there, pretending that I wasn't hauling around a big, grumpy aquatic alien.

Amy took a couple of steps forward and nodded at the aquarium. "That's a lot of calamari you've got there."

Kala-mar-eee? Was that some kind of code word for extraterrestrial? My hands got all sweaty as my grip on the wagon's handle tightened in panic. "Oh, no... it's not, you know, what it looks like... it's not anything... I mean, it's just a squid, a pet squid... er, what does that word mean, exactly?"

Amy laughed. "Relax, Scrub, I was just kidding. Calamari is a fried squid appetizer. It's kind of rubbery, but really tasty."

Uh-oh. Mr. Squid-Man did not like that. He puffed himself up until his head rose all the way out of the water. He opened his mouth to say who knows what, when I put my elbow on top of his slimy head and scrunched him back down into the aquarium. I tried to make it look sort of casual, but I had to lean against that alien with all of my weight. He huffed into the water, sending a stream of bubbles to the surface. Amy watched us, eyebrows raised.

"Oh, right, an appetizer," I said. "That's a good one. Ha-ha." I patted the alien on the head a couple of times in what I hoped looked like an affectionate manner. "We could never do something like that to Grandma's good old family pet here." On the word *pet*, another angry rush of bubbles boiled in the aquarium.

"Of course not. Absolutely out of the question, I'm sure,"

Amy said, sounding much too serious to actually *be* serious. I continued to wrestle with the alien, trying to keep his head underwater. "I can see you've become quite attached to him."

I patted the alien some more. "Yep. I sure have."

"So what's his name?"

"His name?"

"Yes, the name of this pet that you are so attached to."

"Right. His name. He has lots of names, you know? Nicknames."

"Okay. Would you mind telling me one of them?" The question sounded much too innocent to actually *be* innocent.

My mind raced. "Sure...right now I call him...Squidly Bubblemaker."

"That's quite a mouthful. Must be a challenge when you try to call him in for dinner."

"Yeah. Sometimes I just call him Bubbles for short." Where was this stuff coming from?

She nodded. "Good one." Was she trying to hide a smirk?

"Look, do you mind if we change the subject? There aren't many people my age at Grandma's place I can have interesting conversations with, you know?"

"No problem." Amy nodded. "So how have you liked Forest Grove so far?"

"Oh, it's been, you know"—*I discovered the most amazing secret in the history of the Earth! I'm dying to share it with someone and you'd be perfect!*—"pretty good."

Mr. Squid-Man had calmed down, so I eased up on the pressure I was applying to his head. He twisted around in his aquarium and faced the other way. I stepped away from the wagon and exhaled, glad for the chance to pay more attention to Amy.

She was wearing a baseball cap, a pair of pink flip-flops, and a long tank top over a bathing suit. I usually didn't notice girls' clothing, but I sure did with her. I hoped I didn't look too—

"What's all that stuff on your shirt?" Amy asked. I looked down. I had tried to wipe off most of the purple alien spittle, but I saw that it had stained my shirt with several dark blotches. I could feel my face turning the same color.

"Oh . . . that. Right. I just, um, spilled some jelly on myself. At breakfast." Awkward silence. "It happens."

"And it got all over the place on your shirt like that?"

"Um . . . yep."

"Well, I can't say I'm too surprised."

"Really. Why?" Did I look like someone who would be that klutzy?

"We make our jelly with wild berries, and those can be very unpredictable. You're probably not used to that, coming from Florida and all." She said all this with a totally straight face.

"Very funny," I said. Even though I couldn't stop embarrassing myself, something about the look in her eyes gave me the confidence to keep going. "I guess I need a guide, you know? Someone from the area who can show me the ropes so something like that doesn't happen again."

Amy traced a circle in the dirt with the tip of her flip-flop. "Do you have anybody in mind?"

I tapped my finger against my cheek, looking lost in thought. "Let's see . . . I guess you've lived here a long time. Right?"

"All my life."

"And you know the town pretty well, and the people who live here?"

"I'm on a first-name basis with pretty much everyone."

"Perfect. I bet you could give me some great recommendations, then."

She laughed. And this time I think it was *with* me, not *at* me. I forgot all about my chaperoning duties for a second.

Maybe this could work out. Maybe I could actually make a friend in this town. I opened my mouth to try and say something that would make her laugh again—when Mr. Squid-Man sloshed around impatiently in his aquarium, and a wave of water crashed over the side and drenched my face.

I tried to be nonchalant about drying off with the sleeve of my T-shirt, but there really is no smooth maneuver for that. I shot Mr. Squid-Man a quick glare. "He's, uh, he's a little frisky this morning. Heh-heh."

"Maybe he's just trying to help—you know, by washing off all that jelly," she said.

"Ha-ha. You're on a roll this morning."

"Hey, do you mind if I do something?" She held up a set of keys. Hanging from the key chain was one of those tiny digital cameras. "Could I take a picture of Bubbles? He's very colorful."

Uh-oh. My promise to Grandma echoed in my head. I suddenly realized that with this girl's interest in UFOs and books about aliens, it might not be the best idea to have her spend any more time around Mr. Squid-Man. Certainly no pictures. No matter how cute she was.

"No. No, no. That's a bad idea. He's...ummm...shy."

"Oh? Then why are you taking him out in public?" I didn't answer for a minute. "Hmmm?"

"Oh, he, ah, needs to get a certain amount of sunlight each day."

"Really? Sunlight, for a squid?"

"Yeah, he's a special type of squid. From Australia. They live on the Great Barrier Reef, you know, sit up on top of there and get some sunshine, and apparently the vitamin D helps their skin." Wow, I was really babbling now. I wanted to turn things around and put some of the heat on her, ask her why she'd been taking pictures from behind the bushes the day I arrived; but right now it felt more important to put some distance between us. I started pulling the wagon.

"Do you need some help? This is a pretty bumpy trail."

"That's okay." I heaved on the handle and pulled farther away.

"Okay..." She sounded disappointed. "If you ever need any help around your grandma's place, let me know."

I stopped and looked back at her, against my better judgment. "Yeah? You'd help me out?"

"Well, I'd be happy to recommend someone," she called after me.

I smiled and turned to walk down the path. I waved at her over my shoulder as I tugged the wagon as quickly as I could. But as I marched along, my smile faded. As much as I hated to admit it, I was going to have to stay away from that girl.

11

Mr. Squid-Man had his swim in the river—it wasn't too difficult to find a secluded spot where no one would see us—and made friends with a family of beavers building a dam. When he finally returned to shore he looked at me, sniffed wetly, and said, "At least there is one species on this planet that has learned some manners." Then he slid into the aquarium, closed all of his eyes, and started snoring. It took forever to haul him back to the bed-and-breakfast.

After that incident, the rest of the week went much better. I spent nearly all day, every day, GRADEing our alien arrivals. Even though it had to be the strangest summer job in the history of underage employment, I fell into a routine after a while.

And not to brag or anything, but I actually started to get pretty good at it.

I hardly ever had to call in Grandma for backup anymore. Mostly the job was problem-solving through improvisation, and in that way it was like being a good basketball player. I always had to be on my toes and have my head in the game, ready to try a different tactic if the original plan didn't work out. Each situation required some quick thinking and a different strategy, kind of like reading what the defense gives you and then adjusting on the fly.

One time a trio of vacationing alien brothers showed up, each with a pair of devil-type horns growing out of their heads. Luckily, Grandma keeps a trunk of thrift-store clothing in each room. I cut holes in some old baseball caps and slipped them over the horns. They just looked like three goofy guys wearing novelty hats from a joke shop.

Another time a Tourist came through the transporter with orange fur covering every square inch of his body. That GRADE job took a few hours. I shaved the parts of his face that weren't supposed to have hair (nose, forehead, below the eyes) and dressed him up in a long-sleeved flannel shirt, denim overalls, gloves, and boots. He looked like a lumberjack with a bright orange beard, so I figured he'd fit right in around here.

Then came a family of four Tourists with thick tails that reached the floor. For each alien I coiled the tail in a spiral down one leg, tied the tip around the ankle region, and used thick rubber bands to keep it from springing loose. Next I stuffed all of the Tourists into baggy sweatpants and sent them off to start their Earth visit.

There was one time when I got the room numbers switched up and barged in on the wrong Tourists, and they weren't wearing anything at all. (And just for the record, seeing a naked alien is a pretty strange experience. I mean, you know they're naked...but it's impossible to tell which are the bits that are supposed to be covered up, and which are okay for public viewing. I won't go into too much detail here.)

But overall, it was actually kind of a fun job. And Grandma was right. Even though the Tourists acted different and were bizarre-looking, they weren't scary at all. With the exception of Mr. Squid-Man, most of them were pretty friendly, actually. I suppose it's easy to be in a good mood at the beginning of a vacation.

Grandma seemed really happy too. She was always saying how grateful she was to have so much more time these days. And she claimed the Tourists I GRADEd looked more human than most of the people walking the streets of Forest Grove. That wasn't true, of course, but I have to admit it still felt good to hear all that stuff.

And I collected a lot of tips. In fact, I had a whole drawer full of glowing cubes in my bedroom. I'm sure they'd be worth millions of dollars—heck, billions—to any research facility or museum in the world. But I couldn't even use them to buy a peanut butter Twix at the Forest Grove General Store.

One morning, after I finished dressing a group of three-foot-tall aliens in little kids' clothes, someone knocked on the front door. That meant a rare human visitor, of course —maybe the mailman—since the Tourists arrived by transporter.

But what I saw when I opened the door made my heart beat faster than it did during my first GRADE job: yellow baseball cap, brown ponytail, freckled nose, lopsided grin.

"Hi, Scrub," Amy said. "How's it going?"

My stomach went all funny, and a swirl of conflicting emotions took over my mind. On the one hand it was really good to see her, and I was excited that she had stopped by...but on the other hand, the weight of my promise to keep Grandma's secret suffocated me. All I could think about was aliens, the one thing I couldn't talk about. "Oh, it's, you know. Good. Really...good." I just knew that Mr. Harnox was going to walk into the sitting room at any moment, snacking on his tinfoil or smelling the bookshelves, and how would I explain that? I wedged myself into the doorjamb, then pulled the door nearly closed so she couldn't see inside. What was she doing here, anyway?

I think I might have said that out loud, because she looked kind of taken aback. She held up a box with THE ROYAL CHOCOLATE COMPANY printed on the side. "I'm selling candy bars. I know, I know, it sounds kind of lame, but I have to. It's a fund-raiser for a trip to California my school science team is taking in the fall."

We stood there for a minute, looking at each other in silence. She finally leaned forward and whispered, "Now this is when you're supposed to say, 'Why, those look delicious, miss. I think I would like to purchase one of those from you. Or perhaps several.'"

My face got hot. "Sure," I said. If I bought one quickly, maybe she would go away.

She straightened back up. "Great! We're having a special today for out-of-towners and Australian-squid lovers. Seeing as how you're in both categories, it's a super-special for you: only a dollar per bar. You can't beat that."

"Must be my lucky day." I reached into my pocket for some change. But what I pulled out was a handful of alien currency, flashing like crazy. I jammed it back in my pocket, praying she hadn't seen. "Oh, I mean no. No thanks. I don't like chocolate."

"You don't like chocolate?" She frowned. "Well, what about your grandma? Or her customers?" She stood up on her tiptoes and tried to look over my shoulder into the house. "Do you think I could maybe come in and—"

"Nope. Bad idea. Sorry. We're real busy." I backed up and eased the door shut.

"Wait," she said. I paused, peeking out from behind the nearly closed door. Was her face turning red? "I also came by because they're having the Pioneer Day Festival downtown today. The activities are pretty cheesy, but the food is always good. Do you want to come? With me?"

I wanted to, of course, but I had five more arrivals and GRADE jobs scheduled for the next couple of hours.

"Oh, sorry. We're real busy. I, uh, have to work for my grandma. All day. We're real busy."

"You mentioned that."

There was a creak on the floorboards. I turned my head to see a family of greenish Tourists bouncing through the sitting room and up the stairs. Literally bouncing. Amy must not see this. I eased the door even closer toward the frame. "Okay, I should probably go now. Bye." I shut the door all the way and exhaled. Grandma walked through the swinging door that led to the kitchen.

"Who was that at the door, Scrub?"

"Oh, just, you know, someone. A girl. Selling chocolates."

Grandma hurried to the window and peeked out at Amy as she walked back down the road toward town. "Oh, I recognize her. She came here in the spring to interview me for an article she was writing for her school newspaper. The *Independent Businesswomen of Forest Grove*, or some such. We had a wonderful conversation."

"I bet you did."

"She certainly seemed like a nice girl. Very bright."

"Yeah, too bright for this place, if you know what I'm saying."

Grandma ignored that. "She's such a cutie, Scrub. You should have invited her in."

I crossed my arms over my chest. "Grandma, you know that wouldn't be a good idea, right?"

"Oh, nonsense. You're just like your father. I always wanted him to bring his friends over, and he never would."

Can you blame him? I thought.

Grandma nudged me in the ribs with her elbow. "Besides . . . that girl looks like maybe she could be more than just a friend, huh?" She sort of waggled her eyebrows at me.

Gross. "Stop looking at me like that. I'd be worried that she'd see something suspicious, that's all."

"Come, now. I'm sure we can all behave ourselves for at least one afternoon. You should invite her over. Maybe for one of my famous meals, eh?"

But I want her to like *me, Grandma, and I'm not sure your food is going to help.* "I don't know. We'll see," I said.

I certainly had my chances. Amy showed up nearly every day after that, using some excuse or another. One time she was looking to add signatures to a petition asking the city council to renovate the ball fields at the park. Another time she was searching for a lost cat. She even tried the just-stopping-by-for-a-cup-of-sugar trick, though there had to be dozens of houses closer to her own than Grandma's place.

It was impossible to know whether she was stopping by to see me, or if all of that talk about UFOs and aliens meant that she was actually suspicious about what was going on inside here. Man, it's hard enough to know what girls are thinking most of the time without adding interstellar intrigue to the mix.

Even though Grandma usually greeted visitors at the front door herself, she always seemed to be too busy at the moment when Amy came by. Grandma would peek out the window, then say, "Oh, I just remembered I need to run upstairs. Could you answer the door for me, please?" Grandma thought she was good at being sneaky, but she wasn't able to hide her mischievous smile as she hurried past.

So I got to know Amy a little bit better, but only in five-minute snippets of conversation as she stood on the porch while I held the door almost closed, blocking her view of the inside.

But one morning I came downstairs after a rare chance to sleep in, and I was jolted wide awake. There was Amy, sitting with Grandma in the front room, chatting away. Sheets of paper were spread out all over the driftwood coffee table between them.

"Good morning, Scrub," Grandma said. "I was just having a chat with this charming young lady. She walked by the house while I was in the garden and I invited her in. I believe the two of you have met?"

I nodded. My mouth felt too dry to talk.

Grandma stretched and made a big show of checking the watch beneath all of her bracelets. "Heaven and Earth, what happens to the mornings? Already time to make brunch." She stood and motioned to her now-empty seat. "Why don't you sit down, Scrub?"

"Oh, I probably have some work to do," I mumbled.

"Nonsense. Two guests arrived this morning, but I took care of them before you woke up. We have no more scheduled until this afternoon. You actually have a little time to yourself. Isn't that nice?" She patted the seat cushion. And her smile was a little too big as she hurried out through the swinging kitchen door.

Amy flashed me her lopsided grin, and that cluster of freckles on her nose bunched up. "Guess what? I just learned a little secret about this house. Wanna hear it?"

My heart pounded. "A secret? What secret?"

"Promise you won't tell anyone?" She said it slowly, drawing out the suspense.

Oh no. What had Grandma told her? "Of course."

She leaned forward in her chair. "Well . . . I learned"—she glanced from side to side, as if checking for eavesdroppers—"that the front door to this house actually comes *all the way open* when someone named Scrub is not standing there and blocking it with his body. Isn't that amazing?"

I exhaled heavily. "Very funny."

"Yep, it opens right up, and then someone of my approximate size and shape can actually *enter the house*. Who would have thought?"

I wondered how I was going to be able to get her out of here now that she had actually penetrated the Intergalactic Bed and Breakfast's perimeter defenses. I mean, not only was Grandma trying to guard Earth's greatest secret with a white picket fence and a couple of lawn gnomes, but she had just invited in the one person from Forest Grove most interested in her secret.

I looked nervously around the sitting room. Some confused and half-disguised alien could come barreling down the stairs at any moment.

I didn't notice the awkward silence until Amy cleared her throat. "This is the part where you say you're glad I came over," she stage-whispered. "And then you ask me how I like it here."

"Amy, you know I'm glad that you came over." A little awkward silence. "So . . . how do you like it here?"

"Thanks for asking. This place is great," she said. "My house is so plain, it makes me want to scream." She fingered a string of beads hanging from the table. "By the way your Grandma decorates, I can tell we have similar interests."

Okay, that's just creepy. I silently willed her to stop making comparisons between my grandmother and the girl I liked.

"So...what were you two talking about?"

"I was getting her advice about college." Amy indicated the scattered papers.

"You're already thinking about college?" I picked up one of her papers. Printed across the top was *Astrobiology at the University of Washington: A Graduate Certificate Program.* The background showed a bright blue Earth against a starry sky, along with enlarged microscope images of strange organisms.

"What's astrobiology?" I asked.

"The study of life in the universe."

"You mean *alien* life?" The pressure of Grandma's secret felt like a weight on my chest. "They actually have college classes on that kind of stuff?"

"Astrobiology is hard science. Totally legitimate," Amy said, maybe a little defensively.

She was watching me closely, so I tried to keep my voice neutral. "But if no one's ever met an alien, how can you study them?" I was careful not to add, *Unless you spend the weekend at Grandma's.*

"Well, it takes a little imagination to get started," she said. "First off, did you know that some organisms can survive in boiling water? Or within nuclear reactors? Scientists have even found bacteria thriving in toxic-waste sites."

"Okay...so?"

"So let's say you're gathering information about a really hot, wet planet. To us, its surface would basically be like a boiling toxic-waste site, and we'd figure there's no way any life could grow there, right?"

"Yeah..."

"But if we learn about how some types of Earth life, even bacteria, can live in conditions like that, then we might be able to figure out how life grows on those other planets. So you can study life in the universe without ever getting on a spaceship. Pretty neat, huh?"

As usual, I didn't know what to say. Here I was worried about the upcoming FCAT—this test we have to pass in Florida before we can move up to eighth grade—and Amy was already making plans for college.

I had to smile a little, though. With the dozens of aliens I had met in the last couple of weeks, I probably had more astrobiology research under my belt than all of the science professors at the University of Washington combined.

Amy said, "I find it hard to believe you've never wondered about life on other planets. Especially working around here." Why was she saying it like that? Was she testing me? "You've never thought about what aliens might be like?"

I dropped my head to avoid her gaze and mumbled, "Not really." You don't have to wonder about the mysteries of alien existence when you spend the afternoon cleaning their bathroom—the whole idea sort of loses a little bit of the magic after that.

"Well, I think it's fascinating. A great thing about this college program is that I'll get to study all kinds of science at the same time: astronomy, biology, oceanography. Plus a bunch of other stuff. I might be young, but I know this is what I want to do with my life." Amy's cheeks got pink when she talked about something that made her excited. I realized she should probably be working here instead of me.

"And you've been talking to my grandma about all this stuff?" I asked. Amy nodded. Little pinpricks of panic stabbed at my thoughts. Grandma was so accustomed to the aliens that nothing surprised her anymore. She might slip up and accidentally reveal anything during a friendly discussion. "So . . . what'd she say?"

"She was great. Told me she's always been interested in life on other planets, too. In fact, she said that if she were my age, she would plan on doing the exact same thing." Amy's smile faded a bit. "She's a lot more supportive than my dad, that's for sure. And easier to talk to."

I nodded, understanding. Whenever I talked to Grandma she looked right at me, those pink glasses making her eyes huge, and seemed to really think about what I had to say. And, of course, the things we talked about were top secret, and important. So it was different from talking with any other adult. "But I thought you said your dad was the one who got you interested in aliens? Watching movies and stuff?"

"Yeah, but his interest is different. If he ever met an alien he'd probably want to shoot it, not study it. He thinks I'd be wasting my time in college. Says that if I like to talk so much, then I should be a lawyer. Yecch." Amy made a hideous face and rolled her eyes. I laughed. Things seemed to be going okay. Maybe I didn't have to be so stressed out after all.

Grandma glided back into the room. "Well, it looks like you two are getting on well," she said, beaming. "It's time for brunch with some of my guests. Amy, we would be most honored if you could join us."

I moved behind Amy's chair and mouthed *No!* while I made the throat-slashing gesture at Grandma like I was playing a life-or-death game of charades.

Amy turned around to look quizzically at me, and I stopped moving. I glanced at her and then back at Grandma. I swallowed heavily. "Oh, I don't, uh, think that's a very good idea."

"Of course it's a good idea." Grandma and Amy both said this at the exact same time. Scary. They looked at each other and laughed.

Amy stood up, and Grandma took her by the arm and led her down the hallway. It took about three seconds before they were deep in conversation. I sighed, closed the front door, and trudged down the hall after them. As I neared the kitchen, I crossed my fingers. *Please be empty, please be empty, please be empty.*

Grandma pushed open the swinging door. No such luck —the place was packed this morning.

I tried to see everything from Amy's point of view. Grandma's big dining table is L-shaped with seats for more than twenty-five guests, and most of them were filled. The Tourists were disguised, sure, but all together like that they had to look a bit odd to someone who doesn't hang out here every day. And when they all get to babbling together, the sound can be a little unsettling. I figured Amy might be a little hesitant, and I could help control the action.

But she just walked right in and sat down in an empty chair at the middle of the table, near Mr. Harnox and an alien family poring over a hiking map. She helped herself to some scrambled egg substitute from a serving bowl.

"Hello, little ones," Mr. Harnox said as I slid into the seat between them. "It is a morning that is good, yes?"

"Yes it is," Amy said cheerfully. "Good morning to you, too."

"I enjoy how the one sun rises and sets so often in this place," a female Tourist near Mr. Harnox said. Her shoulders were too broad and straight to be strictly normal in the human sense, and her neck was longer than it should be, but I supposed she could pass for an earthling. "At home I feel the loneliness when our suns are darkened for a seeming age."

Amy cast a sidelong glance at me. "She...um...must be from Alaska," I whispered out of the side of my mouth. "You know, one of those towns where it can be night for, like, over a month sometimes."

Amy nodded. "I don't think they have any domesticated squids for pets up there," she whispered back to me, "so I guess we're going to have to find something else to talk to her about." Then she went back to calmly filling up her plate. My heart started beating again.

"These are so very delicious," said one Tourist, pointing to his plate. His skin was really loose, drooping and sagging all over his face. "What are they called?"

"Those are pancakes," Amy said.

I gave a polite laugh, way too nervous, trying to distract Amy from such a strangely obvious question. "Yep, those are pancakes all right!" Amy and the Tourist looked at me, and I smiled much too big. "Mmmm-mmm. Pancakes," I said, too loudly. Amy and the alien exchanged a pitying glance that said they were both aware that there was someone very strange at the table, but they weren't going to embarrass me by saying anything about it.

"And these are also tasty," said the female Tourist. When she opened her mouth to take another bite, I noticed that her tongue was bright green. How could Grandma have missed that during her morning GRADE job? I silently prayed that Amy hadn't noticed.

Amy nodded. "Yes. Those are sausages." She was being very matter-of-fact, but my stomach was still all wonky. This could not last much longer before she got suspicious.

"Made out of tofu," I clarified. Grandma kept all of the Tourists on a strictly vegan diet when they visited Earth. You could never be too careful when it came to alien appetites. She didn't want to give them a bunch of processed food, afraid that the chemicals might mess with their systems. It would be pretty bad PR if enriched riboflavin turned out to be man's greatest weapon against the aliens.

And real meat of any kind was out. What if one of the domesticated pets from their planet—alien's best friend—looked just like a pig, or a cow? It could start up some type of interplanetary incident.

Mr. Harnox scrolled through an electronic book-thing and held it up so the female Tourist could take a look. It was open to a page showing a picture of a soybean plant with some unfamiliar writing underneath. The Tourists all passed the book around, pointing at the picture and chattering excitedly among themselves. I caught a glimpse of the caption on the page: *Plants of Earth*. The weirdness factor was definitely starting to get out of hand, and some holograms could pop out of that alien book at any time. I glanced to my side where, thankfully, Amy was focused on her plate, but still it was getting way too close.

Amy raised her head. She gave a quick glance at me and then addressed the group. "So, you've never eaten pancakes or sausage for breakfast? Where are you all from?"

Yikes. The situation had hit DEFCON One. I had to act immediately, because I sure didn't want anyone here to answer that one. The only idea I had was to fake a coughing fit, but I gave it all I had—pounding on the table, hacking until I was red in the face, the works.

"Scrub, are you okay?" Amy said. She patted me on the back and handed me a glass of water.

"Thanks," I croaked. The aliens were still passing around the book. I had to keep stalling. "So, um, what are you doing this weekend?" I asked.

Amy's eyes lit up. "Oh, I'm so glad you asked. Actually, that's one of the reasons I stopped by today. I'm going to hike along the Nooksack. It has all of these creeks that split off of it, right? Some kids dammed one up at the beginning of summer and made a swimming hole. They even tied a rope swing over it. You can swing right over the pool and drop into the water. It's awesome." Her eyes dipped for a minute; then she looked back up at me, right in my eyes. "I know the water's probably way colder than you're used to, Mr. Florida Sunshine, but do you think you might be able to come? Do you... Would you want to?"

That sounded like a lot of fun. And it would be nice to hang out with Amy somewhere far away from the bed-and-breakfast. But before I could answer, I noticed a Tourist behind Amy, the one with the round head that was too big and the round body that was too little. He was eating his place mat, napkin, and silverware, all piled on top of each other like a sandwich. I had to make sure Amy didn't turn her head—an astrobiologist-in-training might pick up on a clue like that—so I suddenly started gesturing at her with my hands. But I couldn't think of anything to say while I was gesturing, so it was a pretty awkward attempt at a distraction.

Grandma cruised by with a fresh platter of food. When she passed, she lightly swatted the silverware-eating Tourist on the hands. "You stop that now," she whispered. "Just eat the food, please."

"Sorry," he whispered sheepishly. "I thought it was food. It tasted better than that tofu."

I snorted. That alien and I had a lot in common.

"Are you all right, Scrub?" Amy said. I realized that I was still gesturing with my hands.

"Oh, yeah. Great. Everything's great. I was just—uh—practicing my swimming. You know, in case we get a chance to go to that water hole together."

"Okay . . ." She watched me until I stopped gesturing. "So, does that mean you'll come?"

I nodded, much too vigorously. "Sounds like fun." I speared a bit of pancake with my fork and pushed it around the plate, slogging through puddles of syrup. I tried to smile and imitate the quiet calm that Grandma always had, like everything was perfectly ordinary. But then the tofu-sausage-loving Tourist shot her green tongue out of her mouth like a frog, curled it around another link on the serving dish, and sucked it back into her mouth. It only took a split second, but if Amy had seen, it would have been a disaster. Time to end this.

"Whoops!" I said, and knocked over my glass so that milk spilled all over Amy's plate. "Sorry about that! But it looks like you won't be able to finish. Ha-ha! Whoops!" Totally babbling. And there went my chance to make a single human friend this summer.

Amy stood up, using her napkin to mop up the milk that had sloshed onto her jeans. "I'm really sorry," I said lamely.

Grandma came over. "Is everything okay?" she said.

"I think it's time for Amy to go now." I said it pretty forcefully, looking at Grandma and hoping she would pick up on my unspoken meaning. But Amy, of course, took it the wrong way. She looked at the floor and bit her lip; and even I, who knew nothing about girls, could tell she was pretty upset.

I moved toward Amy and tried to salvage part of the morning. "But that hike sounds fun. Really. And the swimming. Maybe we could—"

"It's okay, Scrub. I can take the hint. I know you're busy." Amy finished drying off and dropped her napkin on the table. She looked at Grandma. "Thank you so much for breakfast." Then she walked out of the kitchen through the swinging door.

Grandma watched her leave, then turned to me and put her hand on my shoulder. "I'm sorry, Scrub. I was only trying to help. You've been working so hard, and I thought this morning would be a good chance to take a breather and make a friend."

I shrugged. There was nothing to say. And, okay, so maybe I was a little worried that I might actually start crying or something. The last thing I needed just then was a group of aliens loudly discussing why the earthling was shooting salt water out of his vision cavities.

One of the Tourists held up the *Plants of Earth* page of Mr. Harnox's e-book. "Please for us to try a portion of this for the lunch meal? It looks positively tasty!" The page showed a picture of a giant cactus. Several Tourists clapped their hands in delight.

I shook my head and pushed my way through the swinging kitchen door and down the hall. When I got to my room I flopped onto my bed and stared up at the ceiling. It was a relief to finally be alone.

Now, if only I didn't feel so lonely.

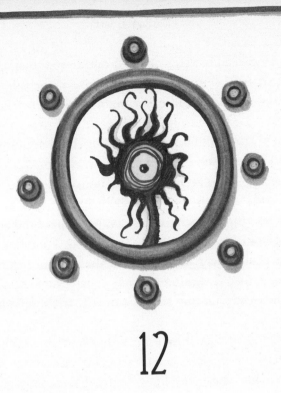

12

After that day, Amy stopped coming by the bed-and-breakfast.

I felt terrible about what had happened, but I didn't know what I was supposed to do about it. I thought about trying to call her, but chickened out. There was even a part of me that was glad I didn't have to constantly make excuses and cover up for the aliens anymore. How lame is that? I mean, I was talking regularly with scaly, sharp-fanged creatures from other planets, but I couldn't even have a conversation with a female of my own species.

I was able to distract myself from these thoughts some-times, though, because we were so busy at the inn. Almost all the rooms were full every night, and there was always lots of GRADEing to do. But I made sure to volunteer for any supply runs into town, half hoping that I might run into Amy in Forest Grove.

One day I was walking to the hardware store, looking down side streets and in every shop window for Amy, when I saw something a couple of blocks ahead that I did not want to find at all.

The sheriff's car was parked at the curb in front of the Pastime Diner. Tate stood beside it, gesturing angrily with his hands and shouting at a pair of very frightened-looking Tourists.

My bloodstream filled up with adrenaline, and I just wanted to turn around and go straight back to the inn. But my annoying conscience knew better. I forced myself to jog right over to the trouble.

When I reached Tate, he had stopped yelling and flailing around. His arms were folded across his chest, and he was chomping on his toothpick. Two squat and boxy Tourists sat on a bench in front of him, clutching each other nervously. I recognized them right away—I had just GRADEd them an hour or so before, and they were really nice. They came to Earth on their honeymoon, they said, "because it's the one place in the universe where we have a zero percent chance of running into someone we know." I could relate. I had felt the same way when I first arrived in Forest Grove.

The sheriff turned and glared at me when I approached. I

froze up for a minute. "Is there something wrong?" I finally said.

Tate didn't move, just stared at me. I looked around his wide belly and gave a little wave to the Tourists. They smiled and waved back, but then snuck a peek at the sheriff and looked back down at the ground.

Finally, Tate stirred. "You bet something's wrong." He took the raggedy toothpick out of his mouth and pointed it at me. "And it's something you could have helped to avoid, boy, if you had any sense."

"What does that mean?"

"You spend any time thinkin' on what I asked you when you first showed up in town?"

"About seeing anything strange or unusual?" I asked. He nodded slightly, then stuck the toothpick back in his mouth and pushed it around with his tongue. "I sure have, sir. And if I do see anything, you'll be the first to know."

Sheriff Tate lowered his sunglasses down on his nose and stared at me. He didn't blink for so long that he could have been one of Grandma's customers, an alien from a planet where eyelids don't exist. He made me uncomfortable, like I had no place to hide my thoughts.

The sheriff nudged his sunglasses back up his nose and shoved a hand into his pocket. When he took it out again it was bunched into a fist, which he stuck in my face and then opened, palm up. He was holding a few coins. They were familiar-looking to me by now. I had a drawer full of them back in my bedroom at Grandma's place.

"These two," he said, jerking his head toward the Tourists

behind him, "tried to buy lunch with these coins at the diner. Now, you happen to know what country these come from?"

I glanced at the coins. "No, sir. I've never seen anything like those before." I swallowed heavily. I wasn't used to talking to law enforcement officials at all, much less lying to them.

"That's funny, isn't it?" he said. But his mouth was so thin and tight-lipped that it was hard to believe it had ever cracked a smile. "I got me a fancy computer right there in my rig, paid for by the good taxpayers of this county just last year." He nodded toward his sheriff's car. Deputy Tisdall sat in the passenger seat, squinting out the windshield and chewing on his upper lip, like a rat. "It's got a hookup to the Internets and everything. I just looked up these coins, and it turns out that *nobody's* seen anything like them before. So whaddaya think of that?" He continued to hold the coins out in his meaty palm, staring like he was trying to look right through me. The aliens cringed behind him. I had to think of something, fast. I remembered the calm, confident way Grandma had spoken to Tate on the front porch.

"Maybe they're counterfeit," I said. It was the first thing that popped into my head.

"What makes you say that?"

"Well...that sign says that the Pastime Diner serves the best meat loaf in the entire Northwest. I guess I can understand how someone might turn to a life of crime to get their hands on some of that," I said.

Sheriff Tate's eyes narrowed and his lips shriveled into a scowl. "Don't you get smart with me, boy," he breathed. I didn't feel so calm and confident anymore. I suddenly became aware of everyone else out on the street. People had stopped walking past us on the sidewalk so they could watch the little show. They were careful not to get too close, but I could feel them staring at us. My face got really hot and it became hard to breathe; it was that disaster of an elementary school play all over again. "I think I should call your grandma down here right now," he said loudly. How embarrassing.

"No, don't do that. She's, um, she's really busy. I'm sorry."

I just wanted to get away from here, get away from that man, and most of all, get away from the heat of all of the people staring at us.

Tate seemed perfectly at ease. "Well, then, what are *you* going to do about this?" I couldn't think of anything to say. "Nothing? I guess I better get in touch with your grandma, then, little fella." He was talking much too loudly, for the benefit of the crowd. Tate turned and called to his deputy through the open window. "Tisdall, get me my—"

"Look, I'll just pay for their meal myself," I said quickly. I fished through my pockets, searching for money. Earth money.

Tate turned back to face me. "You're durn right you will."

"It's all just a misunderstanding," I said. "They're not from around here."

The little crowd broke up, people started walking by again, and the sheriff leaned forward so he could speak to me without anyone else hearing. His voice was soft, but his tone was not. "If you know what's good for you, you'll come clean about what's going on at that Space Place, you hear me? Before it's too late—too late for your grandma, and too late for you." He straightened back up and sneered in the direction of the aliens. "Pay their check and hustle them back to the bed-and-breakfast. I don't want to see 'em again." And with that, Tate squeezed into his sheriff's car and took off.

I had walked the honeymooning aliens halfway to the bed-and-breakfast before my heart stopped pounding. When I made sure they could make it the rest of the way on their own, I turned and walked back into town.

And then I walked past the hardware store, right through town, and out onto the highway that led up to the mountain. I didn't feel like running any errands, and I certainly didn't feel like going back to the bed-and-breakfast. I started kicking rocks as hard as I could, then picked some up so I could nail road signs with them as I passed.

My face was still hot from being humiliated in town, all of those people watching Tate harass me. Why was I always the one getting embarrassed around here? Why did Grandma have to put me in these situations? This would never have happened if I were still at home. I should be hanging out on the beach, not working fourteen-hour days.

I stomped down the highway until my legs ached. I threw rocks until my shoulder got so stiff I couldn't throw anymore. I said some nasty things about Grandma, out loud, to all of the trees that surrounded me; things that I didn't really mean but that felt good to say anyway.

I finally realized this was pointless—it's not like all my problems would be solved once I reached the top of Mount Baker. I sighed, turned around, and plodded back toward Forest Grove.

When I got back into town I looked up at the big clock by the bank. I was going to be two hours late getting to the B and B, but I didn't really care.

I stopped at the pay phone by the diner. If I was already

this late, a few more minutes weren't going to matter, and besides, I needed to hear a familiar voice. I dialed the number to Tyler's cell.

"Hello?" It was hard to hear him; there was a ton of background noise. It sounded like he was in the middle of a parade.

"Hey. Tyler?"

"Hello? Someone there?" He was yelling over the noise.

"Tyler. It's me, Scrub."

"Oh, hey, Scrub. I'm down at the pool." The noise started to make sense now. I could pick out the sounds of splashing, people screaming, and the lifeguard yelling into his bullhorn, "Stay off the rope!" for probably the thousandth time that day. The dull ache of homesickness became a sharper pain. But it was still good to talk to someone I knew.

"How's your summer going?" I said. "Mine's been kind of crazy. I'm working for my grandma. She owns this bed-and-breakfast, and it's really busy. There's a lot of crazy guests." I suddenly smiled, thinking of what Tyler would say about some of the things that came walking out of the transporter. He was always good for a laugh. "It would be great if you were here. I know you'd make fun of some—"

"Scrub? You say something? Didn't hear any of it. Some girls walked by and I had to say hey. You know how it is."

"Oh. Yeah."

"So, what's up? What are you doing out there?"

"Well, I'm—"

"Just a sec, bro." He must have set the phone down on a towel, because the background noise got all muffled. He was gone for so long that I had to pump more quarters into the pay phone. I almost hung up.

Finally, he came back on the line. "Hey. Those girls were over at the ice cream stand. Amanda Peterson was with them. I had to offer some manly assistance, you know? I made all of this money working at one of Coach's little kid hoops camps last week, so now I can afford to buy her stuff. Nice, huh?"

"Yeah."

"Hey, what's the matter?"

"Nothing," I said.

"Nothing, sure. I think I know what's the matter. You know what that bitter taste is in the back of your throat? Let me tell you. It's jealousy, baby. Coach made the roster for the tournament this weekend, and I'm playing point with the starting five. I hope you have that allowance saved up for our bet."

I leaned against the pay phone. "Oh, yeah? Well, there's a park close to here with some hoops. I'm going to work on my three-ball and then—"

"Whoa! Gotta go, Scrub. The ladies are coming over here and I've got some seats saved. Talk to you later."

Click. The line went dead.

I just stood there with the receiver in my hand. I felt like staying out for hours so that Grandma would worry about me and feel terrible for working me so much. I felt like taking the rest of the day off and doing whatever I wanted.

But after I stood there for a few minutes, looking around Forest Grove, I finally realized that I didn't have anything better to do.

I hung up and trudged back to Grandma's place.

13

A couple of days later I got postcards from both my mom and my dad. That would seem like a coincidence to anyone who didn't know my parents. But I could just see them coordinating their e-calendars before they went off on separate business trips. *Monday: Check stock market and adjust portfolio as needed. Tuesday: Conference call regarding the homeowners' association meeting. Wednesday: Communicate with only child via postcard; remember to include term of endearment.*

But I was still feeling a little down, so it was nice to hear from them. I read Dad's first.

Scrub—

I hope the weather is behaving for you up there. I remember one summer, I must have been about your age, when it rained almost every day and barely ever got to 70 degrees (aren't you glad I moved to Florida before you were born?). Give Mother my best and stay out of trouble.

—Dad

P.S. I'm sure you are meeting lots of your grandmother's "eccentric" guests. Has that been the most interesting part of your trip so far?

I read that P.S. over a few times. How much did he know? Everything? Had he ever told Mom? And are there other things going on that I don't even know about yet?

I was really looking forward to having a serious talk with Dad when I got home (and I can't remember ever thinking something like that before).

Then I read Mom's postcard.

Dear Scrub,

I hope you are enjoying your visit to the Pacific Northwest. I have always heard that it's beautiful up there. The seminars are going well here in Jacksonville, but I am eager to be reunited with you and your father. Take care of yourself and I will see you soon.

Much love,

Mom

P.S. I hope that you are getting a chance to throw your basketballs. I know that's important to you.

I smiled. "Throw your basketballs" was such a Mom thing to say. But she had a point. I had been so busy lately that I had almost forgotten how badly I needed some practice. I knew that Tyler had all the advantages this summer and probably had the starting spot wrapped up, but I needed to put up some kind of a fight at least.

And I actually had a couple of free hours this morning. I hadn't said much to Grandma when I got back so late the other day, but I think she figured a few things out, because she told me she would handle all of the GRADE jobs before noon today. With the morning off, I decided to head down to the park and shoot some hoops.

I went out to the backyard first and found Mr. Harnox playing croquet with a newly arrived family of Tourists. I stood on the porch and watched for a minute. Mr. Harnox was trying to play the right way—or at least the *Earth* way —using his croquet mallet and taking his shots in turn. But the other aliens were putting the heavy croquet balls in their mouths, puffing up their cheeks really big, and then spitting the balls twenty or thirty feet through the air. Nobody was taking turns, just firing those balls out of their mouths whenever they felt like it. It looked kind of fun.

I walked out on the lawn, careful to avoid the flying croquet balls, and invited Mr. Harnox to the park. I tried to tell myself that I was doing it as a work-related obligation, but that wasn't entirely true. I mainly invited him so I wouldn't have to go down there alone.

And being there with Mr. Harnox *was* better than shooting hoops alone. Maybe he couldn't dribble, or shoot, or really understand defense, but because he was over seven and a half feet tall, he did serve a purpose. My sixth-grade coach used to hold a broom over his head and make us shoot over it. He said it helped us put arc on our shots, and got us used to playing against taller defenders. So, while Mr. Harnox meandered happily around the court with his hands over his head, I followed, dribbling, and shot over him whenever he happened to wander between me and the basket.

And I even developed a pretty sweet new move, kind of a running, spinning, half-hook shot. I used it to drive the lane and create contact with Mr. Harnox (which would earn me a foul call and a free throw in a real game), and I was still able to get the shot off over his long arms. I worked on that one again and again until I could hit it eight or nine times out of ten.

We were practicing my new move when the high schoolers —Brian, Eddie, and Greg—walked into the park. As they made their way over to me and the tall gray alien, I got so nervous so suddenly that it felt like I was going to throw up.

"Let me do the talking," I said to Mr. Harnox.

"Let you . . . do . . . ?" he said, his brow furrowed in thought.

"Just don't say anything," I whispered as the guys approached.

"Hey, it's Astronaut Scrub," Brian said, bouncing his faded leather basketball. "And he's squidless this time." The three of them stepped from the grass to the asphalt court.

"But he brought a ringer," Eddie said, walking right up to Mr. Harnox. I had thought Eddie was big when I met him the first time, but he looked dwarfish next to Mr. Harnox. "You ever play in the NBA?" Eddie craned his neck back to look straight up at that gray face. The tall alien looked at me and then just shrugged and tried to smile at Eddie. "Nah, you're too old. NBA probably didn't exist when you were young. My great-grandpa has skin that color, and he's ninety-four."

Greg was a few paces behind the others. "Hey, Scrub," he said. "Haven't seen you around much lately."

"Yeah, I've mostly been working at the bed-and-breakfast. We've been really busy." I looked at my watch. "In fact, we should probably be getting back, because pretty soon—"

"Nah, let's play ball," said Eddie. "You wanna play, dontcha, big fella?" Mr. Harnox grinned his hideous grin and bobbed his head up and down. "All right, us three versus you two. That's fair, because he counts for at least two by himself."

"Is that cool?" Greg asked me.

I didn't really have much of a choice. Eddie and Brian were already passing the ball back and forth, playing keep-away from Mr. Harnox, who wandered around in between them. Eddie took a pass, slipped by the alien, and laid it in the basket off the backboard. "Two to nothin'," he said, tossing me the ball and trotting to the other basket.

The game did not go well at first. Mr. Harnox knew enough to run up and down the court, following us from basket to basket, but that was about it. He was so tall that he was sometimes able to keep them from getting a shot off, but mostly that was by accident. I couldn't pass him the ball, either, because he wasn't very good at catching it. I worked myself free to drain a couple of fifteen-foot jumpers, but after about ten minutes Brian announced that the score was twenty-two to four. Eddie laughed. "Is that all? Seems like we're up by way more than that."

After that I planted Mr. Harnox in the middle of the key on defense and told him to just keep waving those long arms in the air. He was a big enough distraction that he forced the teenagers to shoot from the outside, and they went on a cold streak.

On the other end of the court, I used my new offensive move. I drove the lane, jumped, twisted in the air, absorbed the contact from Eddie's leaping body, and then flipped the shot up and over him. I hesitated before my release, making the most of my minuscule hang time, as Eddie swung his arms to try and block my shot. He missed every time. It was way easier than shooting over Mr. Harnox, and I made five in a row.

"Twenty-two to fourteen," I called as I jogged backward down the court to set up on the defensive end. "Looks like we got a game."

Eddie glared at me before he turned to Greg. "Pass it here," he said. Greg waved him off, but Eddie planted himself in front of Greg at half-court. "Give me the ball," he demanded. Greg flipped him the ball and then headed downcourt.

Eddie turned and stared at me. He dribbled the ball much too hard, making a steady *Bam! Bam! Bam!* on the concrete court. I could tell he wanted to run me right over, but Eddie was no point guard. He was too big and stiff, and there was no way he should have been handling the ball this far from the basket. I timed those hard dribbles—*Bam!* pause *Bam!*—and when he started his motion to slam it down the next time, I lunged, poked the ball away, and took off down the court.

I could feel Eddie racing right behind me, heavy footsteps crashing right on my heels. When I got to the hoop I knew he was going to foul me, hard, so I jumped and faked a layup on the right-hand side of the basket. Eddie jumped with me and took a wild swing at either the ball or my head, or both. But I double-pumped the ball, floated through the air underneath the hoop, and flicked it off the backboard on the other side. A perfect reverse layup. Eddie sailed by, his arm swinging harmlessly through the air.

I turned and jogged backward, watching the ball fall cleanly through the net without touching the rim. "Twenty-two to sixteen now," I said.

Eddie grabbed the ball. "That one doesn't count."

"Why not?"

"Traveling."

"I didn't travel!"

"Can't you count? You took, like, four steps. That's traveling. Twenty-two to *fourteen*."

"How could you count my steps? You were too busy chasing me after I stole the ball from you."

Eddie dropped the ball and advanced on me. "I can count the number of seconds it's going to take me to kick your—"

"Guys!" Greg yelled, running to mid-court. "Settle down. It's a pickup game, not the Final Four." He stepped in between me and Eddie. "Let's take a time-out."

My breath came out in a ragged, shaky sigh and I realized that my hands were clenched into fists. Greg pushed on Eddie's chest, and he walked backward off the court, watching me the whole time.

I wiped the sweat off my forehead and huddled with Mr. Harnox while the teenagers chugged sports drinks. The smart thing would have been to just grab him and walk away. The only thing that should've mattered was getting him home safely. The logical part of my brain knew this. But something about the way your blood starts racing in the middle of a game—the sportscasters call it "competitive drive" and Coach calls it the "fire in your belly"—made me forget about what was best. I just wanted to obliterate that stupid look from Eddie's face.

"Can you jump?" I whispered.

"Jump?"

I sort of hopped up and down a few times. Mr. Harnox nodded.

"The next time the bigger one shoots, jump up and smack the ball away." I pantomimed the action.

Mr. Harnox watched me thoughtfully and nodded. "Jump."

"Let's go, ladies," Eddie called. The game resumed. Brian snaked underneath Mr. Harnox's arms for an uncontested layup, and I hit another jumper.

On the next possession, Eddie pulled up for a three-pointer. As a big guy he shouldn't even be shooting out there, but I could tell he wanted to talk some more trash.

Mr. Harnox jumped from underneath the hoop, sailed through the air, and swung clumsily at the ball. It didn't look too pretty, but it was effective. The ball ricocheted off Mr. Harnox's arm and smacked Eddie right in the forehead. It happened so fast that he still had his arms in the follow-through position when the ball nailed him.

Greg and Brian burst out laughing. "Man, you just got *swatted*," Greg said between snorts.

"Yeah, I think he blocked that shot with his *elbow*."

Mr. Harnox looked confused and a little scared. He walked over to me, and I patted him on the arm. "It's okay. That was a nice block. Good work."

"I jumped," he said.

"You sure did!" Greg said, and that sent him and Brian into fresh hysterics.

I fetched the ball and dribbled slowly toward the other end of the court. "What are we playing to, anyway?" I asked as I made my way past the half-court line, facing the defense. Now that Eddie had gotten a little payback, the rational part of me had returned, and I just wanted to get Mr. Harnox home without any otherworldly mishaps.

"What's the matter, can't you handle losing, Space Boy?" Eddie asked.

"Shut up, Eddie. Just play ball," Greg said.

"Don't ever tell me to shut up," Eddie said. He was talking to Greg but glaring at me while he said it.

I tried to use Mr. Harnox to screen the defender so I could take an open three-pointer, but when I slipped around him, Eddie was right there. My momentum brought me crashing into him, and Eddie's forearm jerked up and caught me like a metal bar right in the face.

It hurt so bad that I didn't even notice the pain from crashing flat on my back onto the asphalt. When I sat up and pressed my hand to my nose, blood dripped down my palm.

Eddie towered over me. "Why don't you watch where you're—" he started to say, but then he shot up into the air above me. His legs dangled in the air, kicking wildly, and he choked out a surprised scream.

Mr. Harnox had picked Eddie up by the shirt with one hand, and was holding him at eye level. "Please do no harm to the little one," the alien said.

Brian advanced on Mr. Harnox to help Eddie, but the alien plucked him off the ground as easily as picking a flower. He held the two boys as high and far apart as his long arms would allow. Although the teens thrashed and swore as they hung suspended in the air, Mr. Harnox did not appear to be exerting himself at all. The tall alien simply looked at me, his brow furrowed and the gray skin around his mouth bunched up in a frown.

I stood up quickly. "It's okay, Mr. Harnox, it's okay." I tried to speak in a soothing tone, but I wasn't sure which one of us I was trying to calm down. "Just put them down and we'll go home. All right? Just put them down." I motioned to the ground with both arms, like I was playing charades.

Much to my relief, Mr. Harnox shrugged and let go. The boys fell in a heap on the ground. Brian stayed down, grimacing and rubbing his ankle, but Eddie quickly sprang back up. He backed away from the alien, staring at him, but when Mr. Harnox didn't move, he advanced on me, jabbing his finger into my face. "You little freak magnet. You come here to stay with your crazy grandma, and then you bring some violent psychopath to the park with you? You ought to be—"

Greg stepped in between us, placed both hands on Eddie's chest, and pushed him steadily backward. "You should probably just go home, Scrub," he said to me over his shoulder.

That would have been the best idea, obviously. But I saw a few drops of blood drip onto my shirt, and I got so mad I was back in that red zone again. "No." It was so stupid I couldn't believe it was me saying it. "Let's finish the game. Unless Eddie is too *afraid*."

"I'm not afraid of anything," Eddie snarled.

"Good," I said, and walked over to place the ball in Mr. Harnox's hands. "Put it in the basket," I told him, and pointed at the rim. The alien grabbed the ball and ran toward the basket without dribbling, glad to have something to do. The three teens hustled to get out of the way. He reached up and dunked the ball without even jumping. After the ball went through, Mr. Harnox held on to the rim, wrenching the bolts right out of their sockets and ripping the rim clean off the backboard with a horrible screech. He walked around the court with the orange rim in his hand, looking at it as if he weren't sure what it was or how it had gotten there.

Eddie, Brian, and Greg stared at us with their mouths open. I shrugged. "I guess that's the game," I said.

Now Greg was the one glaring at me. "Thanks a lot. You just ruined our court," he said.

Mr. Harnox took a few steps toward the teens. He probably just wanted to apologize, but they didn't know that. They immediately started walking backward, trying to put distance between themselves and the tall alien. Brian was backpedaling so fast that he stumbled and fell, but quickly pushed himself back up.

Eddie pointed at us. "You won't get away with this," he said. "I will pay you back." Then they all turned and stalked out of the park.

Mr. Harnox handed me the rim. "I make the apology. I do not know how to play this game," he said.

I sighed. "Neither do I."

14

I knelt on the sandy riverbank, rubbing cold water over the dried blood on my face and hands so Grandma wouldn't freak out. My anger had faded, but it was replaced by pure dread. My nerves were on edge as I wondered what the teens were going to do, who they might talk to. I was definitely not looking forward to telling Grandma how badly I'd messed up.

As I tossed rocks out into the middle of the water, Mr. Harnox prowled the edge of the river on his hands and knees. Every once in a while one of his gray hands would dart into the water and come out clutching a wriggling fish. He would show me his catch, give the fish a good sniff or two, mumble a few words to it, then toss it back in the water.

I was about to suggest that we leave when I heard something behind me. I turned, and there was Amy, standing where the grass field of the park met the riverbank. She was wearing her yellow baseball cap, jeans, and a Windbreaker.

"Hey, Scrub."

"Hey." I stood. "It's, um, nice to see you."

"Yeah?" she said, looking at me.

"Of course."

She tilted her head and studied my face. "Are you okay? Your nose looks kind of red and puffy."

I rubbed lightly at my nose. It was still really sore. "I'm fine. I just banged it up a little playing basketball. Took a pass right in the face."

We just stood there for a minute or two in silence. Finally Amy said, "Well, I was just out taking a walk. I'll leave you guys alone." She turned and began walking away.

I hurried over to Mr. Harnox and whispered, "Can you hang out here for a little bit? By yourself? I'll just be right over there, in the park." He nodded.

I ran to catch up with Amy, near the little kids' playground. "Wait up," I said. I glanced back and made sure I could still see Mr. Harnox from where we were standing.

Amy, at the jungle gym, turned to look at me. "You don't have to worry, Scrub. I'll stop bugging you."

"What do you mean?"

She didn't say anything for a long time, just ran her fingers over the crevices of the Goodyear that hung on three chains, one of those twisty tire swings. When she spoke, it was aimed more at the tire than me. "There aren't many people in this town I can really talk to." She stared right at me for a moment. I thought I should say something, but, as usual, I didn't have any words. Her eyes dropped to the swing again. "But I'm sure everybody is way cooler in Florida. So I'll just stop."

My heart beat faster and my mouth got dry. Was talking to girls always this tricky, or only when you were hiding visitors from outer space? And if they can make an alien-to-earthling translator, couldn't they make one that would help me talk to girls?

In a flash of inspiration, I decided to try the truth. Part of it, anyway.

"I thought you were only interested in hanging out with me because of the Intergalactic Bed and Breakfast," I said. "You know, taking pictures, and your interest in astrobiology and outer space and all."

"No way," she said, finally letting go of the tire to look at me again. "I mean, that's part of it, but I hoped it might be something we had in common." She took a few steps over to the regular swings and sat on one, wrapping her arms around the metal chains that held the seat. "But you must not be into that stuff at all."

I swallowed, hard. If only she knew. If we had any chance at being friends, I better try to convince her that nothing was going on at Grandma's place.

I sat on the swing next to her. "I've been thinking about what you said at my grandma's, about astrobiology and extra-terrestrial life and everything."

"Yeah? And?"

"And that's fun in movies, but I don't think it's realistic."

"Why not?" she said.

"I mean, if there is life on other planets, it's probably nothing like life here. It would have evolved under totally different circumstances. We probably wouldn't even be able to recognize it."

Amy smirked. She pushed against the ground with her feet and set her swing in motion, looking much more comfortable now. "You've obviously never studied universal traits in terms of the evolution of physiology."

Yikes. Never try to argue with someone who's way smarter than you are. I sighed, and took the bait. "So . . . what's all that mean?"

"Universal traits. Things that evolution has come up with lots of different times, even on different animals or in different places."

"Huh?"

"Like legs, arms, and eyes. Almost every animal, including humans, has developed some form of them, even in environments that have nothing in common. So we can at least suppose that aliens on different planets might have developed similarly."

I dropped my head so that she couldn't see my expression, which I'm sure was equal parts amazement and panic. Amazement because she had figured out so much on her own, and panic because it was getting harder and harder to keep Grandma's secret.

But Amy must have thought I was trying not to laugh, because she pressed on. "I know, I know, it sounds weird at first. And I'm sure there are lots of differences between humans and aliens. But there have to be enough similarities so we could at least recognize them as fellow beings. I mean, after you've met that Neanderthal Eddie, is it so hard to accept the idea that there just might be beings of higher intelligence out there?" I laughed at that one, and Amy grinned back at me before she turned serious again. "And I bet that we could communicate, too, given enough time."

I glanced over at Mr. Harnox as he bear-walked up and down the banks of the river, trying to communicate with the fish.

Amy sighed. "I should stop talking about this stuff, though," she said.

"Why?"

"Well, if you're not that interested, we can talk about something else. Tell me about where you're from."

We turned our swings around so we were facing each other. I told her about Tampa, and the basketball camp I was supposed to be at, and how I missed being able to swim outside whenever I felt like it. Then she reminded me that I had promised to go swimming with her sometime up at her friends' swimming hole on the Nooksack. I was glad she still wanted to do that.

Amy twisted her swing around and around until the metal chains were locked in a single line, then let go and spun crazily, her arms outstretched. When her swing was totally unwound, she stumbled out of her seat, and our shoes touched. She lurched forward, and I reached out to steady her, grabbing her shoulder and hand.

She looked up at me. "Thanks," she said, and smiled.

When we both sat down on our swings again we were still holding hands.

And then I felt like kissing her. It happened just like that. To be honest, I wasn't even thinking about the Colossal Summer Challenge. There was just something about that little cluster of freckles on her nose, her lopsided smile, and the fact that she was smart and funny and not afraid to talk about the stuff she was into.

And then the nervousness came back, with a vengeance. How would I even start something like that? I couldn't reach her by leaning over in the swing, so I'd have to actually stand up and take a step toward her. And what if she didn't want me to kiss her? Would I just sit back down as if nothing had ever happened? And is it possible to actually die of embarrassment if that did happen?

We sat there, looking at each other and holding hands, and then Sheriff Tate's patrol car cruised into Riverside Park.

"Oh, great." We both said it at once.

"What?" We both said that at the same time too.

"You first," I said.

"I'm in big trouble," she said.

"Me too."

Sheriff Tate bumped his car over the curb, drove right out on the grassy field, and pulled up broadside to the playground equipment. He rolled down his window and leaned out. "I thought I told you not to come down here," he said. I was about to open my mouth to answer him when—

"Da-ad!" Amy said. She dropped my hand, jumped out of the swing, and jogged toward the car.

My jaw must have fallen below my waist.

Amy walked around to the other side of the car and opened the door. "You're embarrassing me," she hissed to her father.

"Never mind that. You climb in. They're waiting on us, and you're making us late." Before she got in, she looked at me over the roof of the patrol car and mouthed, *I'm sorry.*

Sheriff Tate glared at me. "Some boys just told me an interesting story," he said. "About a little dustup down here with you and one of your grandma's whacked-out customers. Said you two attacked them."

I couldn't find my voice to protest. I just stared at the car, Amy's sad face framed by the window.

"I just made closing down your grandma's place and shipping you out of town my first priority, boy. You'll be seeing me soon." Tate gunned the engine and sped out of the park.

15

I don't remember walking back to Grandma's. My mind was too busy figuring out what to worry about most: the possibility of getting revenge-jumped by high schoolers, Sheriff Tate's threat, or losing the only friend I had in this town. So many things had gone so wrong, I couldn't muster up much emotion for any one of them. I just felt numb. Then there was the problem of what to tell Grandma. She'd been running her business safely and secretly for over forty years, and I had messed up everything in just a few weeks.

My feet figured out the way home by themselves, though, because suddenly I was trudging up the front steps of the Intergalactic Bed and Breakfast, Mr. Harnox following.

"Do you sense the empty feeling inside of you?" he said.

What? Was he reading my mind or something? Could they do that on his planet? "I do," I said, without even really thinking about what I was doing. Oh, man, was I actually about to pour out my secrets to an alien? Could he actually—

"Because I am experiencing the emptiness inside of me." Mr. Harnox patted his belly. "The empty-stomach-hunger feeling that signals a need for the half-day meal."

Oh, it was just that. "I went shopping yesterday. There's a fresh pile of tinfoil and some bottles of bleach on the kitchen counter." I watched him nod happily. "I got you the Jumbo Family Pack this time."

Mr. Harnox grinned hugely. At least I was able to make one person happy.

I pulled open the front door. Mr. Harnox walked past me, heading for the kitchen. I looked around and saw that a jungle was growing in the sitting room. I didn't miss a step, just walked inside; I guess I was getting acclimated to the weirdness of this place.

With a second glance I realized it was only a couple of giant aliens having trouble fitting into their new surroundings. And giant is no exaggeration. The ceiling in Grandma's sitting room is as high as a basketball hoop, and the aliens' heads brushed up against it. Well, not their heads, exactly, but they had these weird growths—antennae, maybe, which were broad and green and looked kind of like the fronds on a palm tree—sprouting out of the top of their heads. Their bodies were brownish and tube-shaped and speckled with various shades of green and yellow. Adding to their rainforest look were long arms and legs, each ending in a dozen or so plantlike tendrils.

After a few moments of staring, I realized that even though their heads reached the ceiling, they were actually sitting down with their knees scrunched up and their backs hunched over. If they stood up they would easily be taller than the house. Even though the Tourists seemed to take up the entire room, Grandma found a small clearing and stood right in front of them, looking up at the huge creatures. She crossed her arms over her chest and shook her head.

"I'm terribly sorry, sir. We try to welcome everyone here, but I'm afraid it's just not possible."

"But the *Intergalactic Travel Guide* doesn't list any height restrictions for Earth travel," one of the giant aliens said in a deep, rumbly voice. He attempted to make a gesture while he spoke, but his arms were so long they scraped against the walls, sending a few framed pictures crashing to the floor. "Sorry about that," he muttered.

"I am aware that the *Guide* contains incomplete reports," Grandma said. "But I simply cannot let you step out of this house. In fact, you should not even be on the ground floor without an Earth disguise. Although in your case, I can't imagine what that would be."

"I assure you we have no intentions of speaking with the natives," the other giant alien said. "Couldn't we at least stroll around for a few hours? Perhaps no one will even notice us."

I was pretty impressed with Grandma. Those aliens could have scooped her up and polished her off in one bite, but Grandma didn't back down.

"Oh, for the Creator's sake," she said, hands now planted on her hips. "You two are at least ten times as large as the average earthling. And unfortunately we are still a single-species operation down here when it comes to what passes for higher intelligence. You would be noticed immediately."

"But couldn't we—"

"And furthermore," Grandma interrupted, "if you get caught and your arrival is traced back here, I lose my Interstellar Hotelier License. Permanently. I would have to shut down the entire business. The *Guide* might be incomplete on some things, but it is quite clear regarding that matter."

The aliens looked at each other. They might have shrugged their shoulders, but I'm not sure—it's hard to tell where the shoulders are on giant, living, jungle trees. "The children will be terribly disappointed," one of them said.

Crash! Something barreled down the stairs, a confused blur of color and noise. More pictures fell off the wall as it thudded down each step, and a couple of wooden balusters shook free from the railing. The something fell all the way to the landing and smashed into the wall before I could even tell what it was: a tangled mass of three aliens with the same color and shape as the giants, only on a much smaller scale.

One of the creatures—he looked to be about my height—was the first to recover. He jumped up, grabbed one of the others by the palm-frond-thingies on top of his head, and smacked him in the face with a skinny branch-arm. The third alien, flat on his back, shot out the tendrils at the bottom of his legs and wrapped them around the lower torso of the attacker and pulled, sending him crashing to the floor again. Then the two aliens on the ground jumped up and tackled the first one, pinning him to the ground and thumping him all over.

"Children! Enough!" roared one of the giant aliens. "You are guests on this planet and you will behave yourselves!"

The kid aliens untangled themselves, stood up, and stared at the floor. "Sorry, Mom," one of them mumbled.

The mother alien looked at Grandma. "You'll have to excuse my boys. They have a tendency to be a little... energetic."

The father alien pointed to the kid who had apologized. "I'm especially disappointed in you, Zardolph. As the oldest, your brothers look to you for guidance."

"But, Da-a-ad," Zardolph whined. "It's too boring to be inside. The gravity is so light on this planet you can jump forever. Can we go outside and play? Pl-e-e-e-ase?" The other two nodded, their palm fronds bouncing wildly.

"I'm afraid we have some bad news," the mother alien said. "We have to leave immediately."

"No-o-o-o!" the alien kids howled. They dropped down and hammered their branch-arms on the floor, their palm fronds a tangled mess as they shook their heads fiercely. Apparently Earth toddlers didn't invent the temper tantrum.

"It seems we are not welcome on this planet," the mother added, looking at Grandma. "And this vacation would have been such a nice present for your birthday, Zardolph." The tantrum grew louder.

"Stop that right now!" the father alien yelled. The aliens stopped beating on the ground but remained lying down.

"But we've been looking forward to this vacation all year. School starts in three days," Zardolph said.

"Yeah, and then we won't have any fun at all!" said one of his brothers.

"It's not fair!" cried the third. They all started wailing again. Grandma tried to say something to the parents but was drowned out by the group tantrum.

I crossed to Grandma. "Need some help?" I had to raise my voice over all of that noise.

Grandma leaned closer. "I need to talk to the parents, but I can't hear myself think."

I held up one finger and ran up the stairs to my room. I pulled the little Nerf hoop off the wall by my bed, grabbed the ball, and rushed back downstairs.

"Listen up!" I yelled to the three brothers. They all stopped thrashing around and stared at me. "You guys wanna play an Earth game?"

Zardolph glanced at his slightly smaller brothers, then looked at me and nodded.

"You said you liked to jump, right?" I said, and he nodded again. "Follow me."

I led them over to the bookcase, Grandma and the huge aliens watching. Using the shelves as a ladder, I scrambled up and stuck the hoop as far up the wall as I could manage. Then I dropped back to the floor. "Okay, the game's called Put The Ball In The Basket." The three young aliens crowded around me, all of them trying to snatch the ball out of my hands. I held it over my head and brushed them aside with the other hand. "Whoa. Wait a minute. Line up. Stand one in front of the other. There, like that. Now—it's Zardolph, right? It's your birthday, so you get to go first."

Zardolph stepped forward and grabbed the ball. He took a run at the wall, bounced off it, rebounded against the bookshelf, and hit the wall again, higher up this time. He ended his routine with a flip on the way to the basket, where he dropped the ball through the hoop.

"Hey, nice moves," I said.

He collected the ball and ran back to me, smiling. "Earth is awesome! That's twice as high as I can jump at home."

Grandma smiled and waved at me, then resumed her conversation with the parents. I taught the kids reverse dunks, 360s, and threw them some alley-oop passes. It was actually kind of fun.

After a few minutes Grandma called us all over. "I think we may have come up with a plan," she said to the kid aliens. "I'm afraid your parents are simply too big to stay here. I am quite firm on that point." The kids moaned. "But perhaps you three could stay for one night." The moans turned to cheers. The kids scampered over to their parents and tugged on their massive arms.

"Can we stay? Pleasepleasepleaseplease? Can we?" They all talked over one another.

The giant aliens looked at each other. "I don't know... they've never been on their own before...."

"My grandson Scrub here is working for me this summer, and he is a fine young human. Perhaps he can take the children out for an overnight camping trip." The kids started a fresh round of begging, but Grandma cut them off. "They won't be able to go near the town or any houses, or meet any of the natives, but they will still have fun playing with Scrub outside in a genuine Earth forest."

Oh no.

I tried to catch Grandma's eye, shaking my head and making the throat-slashing gesture, but she was beaming at the aliens and didn't notice. This was a terrible plan. And so unfair that she would just blurt it out like that without even thinking, or asking me.

The giants looked at each other, then down at their kids. "Well...I guess that might be acceptable." The kids jumped up and down, squealing. "But we'll be back tomorrow morning to pick you up. And you need to be on your best behavior, do you understand? Now, go thank your new friend."

The Jungle Boys swarmed over me. I stuck out my hand for them to shake, but instead they rubbed their palm fronds all over my face. It didn't hurt, but it was slimy and sort of suffocating. They all chattered at me at once. I couldn't really tell what they were saying, but I got the idea they were excited about the camping trip. Finally, Grandma waded through the aliens and escorted me down the hall.

We stopped just outside the kitchen door. "I realize this is a lot to ask, Scrub."

I looked away, glared at the wall. "Yeah. It is." Especially after the morning I'd had.

"But it will mean so much to those boys."

"You could have at least asked me first before you announced it to everybody."

Grandma put her hand on my shoulder. "Oh, Scrub. You're

right, of course. I was only thinking of myself and the best way out of that situation. Please forgive me."

I looked at Grandma. It was the first time that an adult had ever apologized to me. I took a deep breath, and nodded.

Grandma gave me a hug. I was sort of getting used to that. "I'm afraid that I'm taking you for granted already. It's just that I could never have handled an emergency like this before you got here. You're the best employee I've ever had."

"I'm the only employee you've ever had."

She smiled. "To be honest, I'm not sure how I ever managed without you."

It felt good to be useful around here, to be needed.

Mr. Harnox walked out of the kitchen and past us then, smacking on his tinfoil. He gave us a little wave as he walked by and headed up the stars. My anger disappeared when I saw him, as I suddenly remembered the bad news I had for Grandma.

I turned from her gaze and looked down the hall, where the parent aliens were trying to corral their kids. A near-impossible task, as they were so squished up in the sitting room.

I stalled my confession with a question. "How did those giants even get through the transporters?"

"There's one in the basement that's a bit bigger. They crawled out headfirst and just kept coming and coming. Like watching a hundred clowns pop out of a single car at the circus." Grandma giggled. "You know, it would almost be worth getting caught just to see the look on Sheriff Tate's face when he met those two. I'd like to see him try to bully a couple of giants. He'd probably swallow that awful toothpick."

139

Grandma was really laughing now, but at the mention of the sheriff, a cold lump of dread formed in my stomach. "Look, Grandma, speaking of Tate...I don't mind helping you out with the kids, but I don't know if leaving the house on a camping trip is such a good idea."

"Why is that?"

I told her the story, looking at the ground and talking as quickly as I could to get it over with. I ended with how Sheriff Tate threatened to shut down her place, and wondered if she was still going to talk to me after that.

She did. "Oh, dear. You must feel fairly shattered with worry. I'm as sorry as can be."

"I'm the one who should be sorry."

"It's no fault of yours, Scrub, and never were words more true."

"But what do you think the sheriff is going to do?"

Grandma shook her head and scoffed. "If we act scared, then that bully has already won. We are simply not going to let someone like that run our lives."

"I guess..."

"And besides, if he's sniffing around here and doing his endless cruising around town, it might be good to get yourself and our guests to a secluded spot in the woods." Grandma put her soft hands on either side of my face. "Will you do this for me?"

I shrugged, and nodded. Grandma had a point.

"Oh, Scrub. Thank you and bless you. You're the best. Even better than the first sunny day after a gloomy Northwest winter."

She gave me a kiss and hurried back down the hall. Then it dawned on me: I had been so worried about everything else, I forgot all about the most important obstacle. I had never been camping before.

16

It took most of the afternoon to rummage through Grandma's backyard storage sheds, gathering scattered bits of camping equipment. I had to wade through forty years' worth of stuff: stacks of yellowing newspapers, boxes of Christmas decorations, half-used cans of house paint. Apparently she never threw anything away.

When I finally had everything crammed on top of the Radio Flyer wagon and bungee-corded into place, I checked back inside. The alien parents had left, and Grandma was finishing up disguising the

Jungle Boys in the sitting room. "Well, Scrub, it might not be perfect, but it should be good enough for a night in the woods, am I right?"

Yikes. "Might not be perfect" was kind of an understatement. She had gathered up the palm-frond-thingies on top of each alien's head and wrapped a headband around them, so it sort of looked like they had dreadlocks . . . but not really. They were stuffed into baggy sweatpants and long-sleeved baseball shirts that weren't quite able to hide the tubular shape of their bodies, and the long tendrils that stuck out of the sleeves sure didn't look like fingers. And although the brown coloring of their flesh was a normal earthling tone, it would be hard to explain those camouflagelike splotches of green and yellow. We'd have to stay very well hidden on our little excursion.

The Jungle Boys bounced all over the room—leaping over the couch, doing those impossibly high jumps to peek out the upper windows, tackling each other and rolling around on the carpet. They were a cross between kindergarten boys on a sugar binge and a pack of wild puppies.

"They certainly have a lot of spirit, don't they, Scrub?"

"Uh, yeah. They do." I was honestly starting to wonder whether hundreds of square miles of forested wilderness was going to be enough space to contain them.

"I packed up some goodies for the evening." Grandma handed me an old-fashioned wicker picnic basket. "There are some tofu dogs and whole wheat buns, as well as couscous salad. And fresh carrot juice in the thermos. Oh, and I put in all the fixings for good old s'mores. Perfect for camping. When the boys taste one of those treats, they may never want to go back to their home planet again." Grandma giggled at her little joke. I tried to muster up a courtesy smile for her, but I knew I'd probably be eating graham crackers for dinner and marshmallows for breakfast. While I appreciate the fact that Grandma cooks every day...I'm still not sure I'll ever get used to the actual food she comes up with. With any luck, the kids from outer space would eat the New Agey stuff.

"Oh, and take this, just in case." Grandma handed me a dog-eared copy of a book called *So You Think You Can Camp? A City Slicker's Guide to Outdoor Fun in the Pacific Northwest.* I flipped through the pages and it looked like one of those "moron manuals" for first-timers. "This should answer any questions you might have."

While the aliens whirled around us, I peeked out the window. Thankfully, the street was deserted. Grandma hugged me good-bye; then I rounded up the little Tourists and we headed off.

We made a mad dash to the end of the street, me pulling on the handle of the wagon and the Jungle Boys pushing the back end to help get us quickly onto the dirt road that disappeared into the forest. Once we were behind the cover of trees, I started to feel a little better; and when we branched off on a trail that led even deeper into the wilderness, it felt like a weight had been lifted from my chest. My troubles would still be waiting patiently for me when I returned to Forest Grove, but maybe Grandma was right: a little time away would be good.

Before long I was dragging the wagon by myself, as it was impossible to keep all three aliens on the trail. A squirrel would scurry by and disappear into the underbrush, and they would tear off after it, crashing through thickets of fern bushes. If the alien in the lead tripped and fell down, the other two would run right over his back. And they had contests to see who could touch the highest tree branch, taking running leaps at limbs that were easily twenty or thirty feet off the ground. Sometimes they slammed into each other in midair, or grabbed a dying branch that snapped clean off its tree and sent them crashing to the ground.

At first I was pretty freaked out by all of their crazy exuberance—what if they impaled themselves on a tree branch or broke an arm or something? It's not like I could take them to the hospital, or even the veterinarian's. And I sure didn't want to be the one to explain to those giant parents that I had let something horrible happen to their kids. But the little aliens seemed to be made of rubber; they just bounced off any obstacle and kept running. Nothing hurt them or shook them up that much.

The cloud cover from earlier that morning had broken up, and it turned out to be the first really warm day since I had arrived. It was almost five o'clock, the warmest part of the day here, and after dragging the wagon around, I found the temperature bordering on hot, even.

We hiked until my legs ached, and finally we heard the muted roar of white water as the trail met up with the Nooksack River. I had avoided the river trails near Grandma's place and Forest Grove—too many potential hikers around there—but I figured we were deep enough in the wilderness to safely join the Nooksack again.

The forest grew right to the edge of the river, small trees and blackberry brambles hanging out over the water. We walked along the trail, which now followed the natural curves of the river. Sometimes we came to clearings that allowed us to walk down to the water's edge, the ground here completely covered with smooth white river stones the size of footballs. We stopped at one of these, and I taught the aliens how to skip a flat rock across the surface of the river. Their fingers—or digits, or tendrils, or whatever you wanted to call them—were perfect for wrapping around the rocks, and they unfurled with a snap to send the stones skipping all the way across the Nooksack.

Those aliens sure liked to play in the water. Actually, they liked to play *on* the water; they were able to splay their feet-tendrils into flippers, and with a running start from the riverbank they could run on top of the water for a while. They chased each other, feet slapping against the little white ripples that formed as the water churned over the rocks, until gravity caught up with them and sucked them underneath the surface. At first I was nervous they were going to drown, but the river wasn't very deep, and they always came bounding out onto the riverbank, shaking themselves dry like dogs.

Lots of trees had fallen into the water, creating natural bridges. The aliens liked to chase one another on these as well, running down the length of a trunk with scary good balance, then jumping off and diving into the bushes to hide from each other.

For all of their energy and crazed activity, I had to admit they were pretty well-behaved. Every time I yelled to them that it was time to get on the trail, they ran back to me without any argument. It was weird to tell aliens what to do; I felt like a babysitter. I kept expecting them to get tired and lie down on the riverbank for a rest, but they never seemed to run out of steam.

I was getting plenty tired myself, though, pulling that stuffed wagon over the exposed tree roots that crisscrossed the trail like huge pythons. After lugging our gear through the woods all this way, I figured we were far enough away from civilization to start looking for a place to set up camp.

But what was that? The river was calm here, more murmur than roar, and I thought I heard something. "Shhhh! You guys, be quiet. Now!" I stage-whispered. The Jungle Boys froze. I leaned forward, straining to pick up a noise, my heart seeming as still as the aliens.

There! A burst of sound—a laugh, or maybe a cough. And then a bit of a song, the words unclear, but the tune floating over the sound of the water. It came from straight ahead, where the trail followed a bend in the river and disappeared from sight. Someone was headed our way. Maybe a bunch of someones.

I looked around frantically. My heart started back up and was beating way too hard. In front of us was a clear area of the forest, not much underbrush to use as cover and lots of open space between the trees. A thicket of blackberry brambles grew between us and the water, but there was no way we could wedge ourselves in there. It was way too dense, and I'd be a bloody mess if I tried that.

Nowhere to hide.

Our only option was to run back down the trail the way we had come, but we'd have to ditch our gear to get any speed.

Besides, the trail was a straight shot behind us; whoever was coming would be around the curve in the path soon and would certainly see us.

"Quick, you guys, over here!" I stepped off the trail, getting closer to the blackberry thicket and shielding us from sight behind a couple of trees. They would give us partial cover from this distance, but when the group walked by on the trail we would be totally exposed.

I peeked from behind a tree, my cheek pressed against the rough bark. The bend in the river was about half the length of a football field away. Someone walked around the curve, stepping into view. I shielded my eyes from the sun, squinting for a better look. And no, there's no way it could be—

But it was. Sheriff Tate, walking down the trail. Wearing his uniform and carrying a huge hiking stick.

I whipped my head around and stood with my back jammed up against the tree. "Get down!" I whispered to the aliens.

I scanned the area—my head on a swivel, checking every square inch of our surroundings—as if that would miraculously make a hiding place appear. My knees got jittery and sweat dripped from my forehead to sting my eyes. My brain decided to get lost inside a cloud of panicky thoughts instead of helping me find a way out of this. *What have I done? How did Tate find us out here? What will he do to me out here in the wilderness? He'll be here any second and he'll find us and there will be nothing that I can say to try to explain it rationally and Grandma will lose her business and WHAT AM I EVEN DOING HERE IN THE FIRST PLACE???*

The aliens huddled around me, wordlessly picking up on my fear. They peered all around, looking at each tree, their eyes opening and closing rapidly and their bodies shaking. Seeing things from their perspective helped me get myself under control. How scared would I be if I were on another planet and suddenly my guide lost it and started acting like a total spaz? I thought of the promise I had made to Grandma and knew it was time for me to act. "Come on. Don't be a screwup," I muttered to myself.

"Don't be what?" one of the aliens said.

"Never mind. Take off those clothes, quick!" I whispered. I shoved the wagon over to a cluster of knee-high fern bushes and dumped it over on its side, spilling the camping gear behind the green leaves. The bushes did a decent job of hiding our gear, but as they stood only a couple of feet high, they weren't nearly enough cover for the four of us.

I could hear separate voices now but couldn't make out the words. What was Tate doing out here with other people? Was it a search party, looking for us?

The Jungle Boys peeled off their sweatpants, T-shirts, and headbands. "Give them to me!" I said, and threw their clothes into the ferns with the camping gear. Tate and his posse were close enough that I could hear the sticks snapping under their feet. We only had a few seconds before they walked right by our little clearing. I moved in very close to the aliens. "Okay, listen to me," I whispered. "You need to close your eyes and just stand there, perfectly still, like this." I pressed my legs together and stuck my arms out at different angles. They copied me, and I felt a brief spark of hope that this might actually work. "That's great. That looks great. Now, whatever happens, don't move. Okay? And don't say anything until I tell you to. That's very, very important. *Don't move.*"

I ducked behind them and scrunched myself up as small as I could. There was a slit of daylight between the aliens, enough for me to use as a peephole to watch the trail.

Tate walked into view, only a few yards from where I was hiding behind the Jungle Boys. I felt horribly exposed. Walking right behind Tate were Eddie, Brian, and Greg. And to my horror, they were wearing uniforms too.

That's it, I thought. It's over. If Tate is actually going to deputize teenagers and hunt us down in the forest, then there's nothing I can do. It's over.

But before I could think about surrendering or praying for mercy, I saw more people walking into view behind the high schoolers. There were about a dozen of them, and they were just kids. Maybe nine or ten years old.

I shifted my position, blackberry thorns digging into my back, and took a closer look at Tate. He was wearing a uniform, all right, but it wasn't his usual sheriff's uniform. It was some sort of Scout troop leader getup. The smaller kids had dark blue uniforms—I remembered them from the one year that Tyler and I tried Cub Scouts—while Eddie, Brian, and Greg wore tan-and-green uniforms. Probably Eagle Scouts, at their age.

My muscles relaxed a bit and I exhaled. It must have been the first time in quite a while, because I almost fell over and passed out. This was still a close call, but I'll take Cub Scouts over grown-ups with guns and bloodhounds any day.

Besides, it looked like they were all going to just walk right by us anyway. Hopefully the aliens were blending in with the tangle of foliage behind us. I crouched into a little ball again.

The group filed slowly past us. All of them were wearing heavy-duty backpacks with a sleeping bag attached to the top. The long brown stock of a hunting rifle poked up out of Tate's pack and extended over the top of his hat.

All of a sudden Tate stopped, and the whole line of Scouts halted behind him. Tate looked around the forest, then backtracked a few steps. I held my breath again.

"Now, boys, be sure to write this stuff I'm telling you down in your nature journals," Tate said in his slow drawl. "This here's a cedar tree. You can tell by the stringy bark." He stepped off the trail, getting even closer to us, and patted a tree. "This is a western red cedar, if you want to get specific. Cedars were the most useful tree for the Indian tribes around here, years ago." Tate peeled off a short length of the bark and held it up. "See this? They could weave this bark into hats, baskets, all manner of things. And did I ever tell you boys what a hardy and durable tree this is? A healthy cedar can live to be over one thousand years old."

"What a coincidence. He's told us that over one thousand times," Eddie muttered to his buddies. Brian and Greg snickered.

"What's that?" Tate asked.

"Nothing, sir."

Tate moved on to another tree, his back turned to us as he faced the Scouts. "And this here? It's a bigleaf maple. This is a deciduous tree, so those leaves will fall off in autumn, unlike the conifers, or 'evergreens,' like all of these Douglas firs that keep their green needles all year round. Pay attention to your troop leader now, and hopefully some of you will be able to earn a wilderness badge when we're finished up out here tomorrow."

Just when I thought they were going to move on out of sight and I could start breathing normally again, one of the kids pointed straight at the aliens. "What kind of trees are those?" he asked.

Perfect. Just my luck, to get stuck with the little Scout who wanted to bypass the wilderness badge and go straight for his space alien identification badge.

I watched through the slit between the aliens, not daring to breathe, as Sheriff Tate strolled up to the Jungle Boys. He came really near us, studying the "bark." He got so close that his belly, which plopped right over his belt, was pressing up against Zardolph. I was afraid that he'd hear me breathing.

And was Zardolph moving? His torso slowly slithered away from Tate. I thumped him in the back to remind him to stay still, and prayed he would remember to keep quiet.

Tate squinted up and down the length of the "tree," that soggy toothpick lolling from one side of his mouth to the other. "Hmmmm. What have we here?" he muttered. He ran his hand over one of the Jungle Boys' arms, and I prayed that aliens weren't ticklish. "What indeedy do we have right here?"

Some of the scouts behind Tate elbowed each other in the ribs and smiled. "What's the matter, Mr. Troop Leader, sir?" Brian said. "Don't you know what kind of tree that is?" The smiles grew wider all around.

Tate stepped away from the aliens. "What? Oh, no, of course I do. Of course I do."

A few boys pulled out their nature journals and stood there looking at Tate innocently. "Could you please tell us, sir? So we can write it down? In detail?" Eddie said.

Tate took one more hard look. "These here are madrona trees, boys." He stepped forward and gave one of the aliens a few hard taps. "Yep, madrona trees, mark my words. I've lived here all m'life and I'd know a madrona tree anywhere. They only grow in the Pacific Northwest. They're usually found by the coast, but occasionally you see them near fresh water. Good-looking trees, eh, boys?"

"Yes, sir," a few of them mumbled. They tucked their journals back into their packs, clearly disappointed that this session of stump-the-troop-leader hadn't worked out.

As Tate returned to the trail, he glanced back over his shoulder at the "trees," his eyebrows lowered and a scowl on his face. He hesitated for a moment, and I almost thought he was going to walk back for further inspection. I held my breath.

Finally he turned back and joined his Scouts on the trail. I let out another relieved sigh, and my legs went so watery I nearly fell over.

My relief didn't last long. "Can we set up our campsite here, Mr. Tate?" one of them asked. "I'm tired."

"Yeah, me too."

"We've been hiking out here forever."

Tate surveyed the area. What would we do if he stayed? No way did I trust the Jungle Boys to stay still much longer.

"Nope," Sheriff Tate said. A chorus of groans rose from the group. "Now look here, boys. There's a clearing just up the hill from the riverbank a little ways down the trail. We'll set up camp there. Be easier to fetch water and find driftwood for our campfire." There was some minor grumbling. "It'll just take a few minutes to get down there. Now, are we real Scouts, or what?"

"Yes, sir," some of the boys mumbled.

"Then let's get a move on."

This time I held my breath until they were down the trail and out of sight. I finally exhaled and started shaking all over.

"That was great, you guys. I'm really proud of you."

The aliens all spoke at once, babbling over each other and biting off the ends of each other's sentences.

"—my arms were so tired that I—"

"—did you see how close he got to me, with his big belly pressing—"

"—his breath made my eyes water when—"

"—did he actually think we were one of these Earth plants that—"

"—I had the worst itch when—"

I finally quieted them down. Tate may have been gone, but that didn't mean he would never come back.

"Come on, you guys, we should probably put some distance between us and those Scouts before we make our camp." I pushed the wagon back on its wheels and piled on the camping gear. When I got back on the trail, the Jungle Boys were already racing ahead of me.

I sighed. Not only did I have to keep these three rowdy

aliens alive, but they had to stay hidden from the suspicious sheriff and a dozen curious Scouts.

Somehow I didn't think I would find any helpful tips in Grandma's copy of *So You Think You Can Camp?*

17

It took forever to get the big tent set up. I tried to consult the beginner's camping book, but it was way too complicated. Apparently I needed a manual aimed at whichever skill level was just below "moron."

Sometimes I wish they would teach practical skills in school. Setting Up Tents 101, maybe, or Talking to Girls: A Course for Beginners.

But you have to learn the useful stuff by actually doing it yourself. So I wrestled with tent poles and layers of canvas until they resembled something that you could crawl inside of and would maybe keep you dry while you slept.

Zardolph and his brothers didn't make things any easier. They tried to help for five minutes or so, but then a family of deer wandered by, and the Jungle Boys chased them around our clearing. I had never seen deer up close before. They could do these cool jumps where they sailed through the air, then landed for just a split second before they shot back into the air again, like they had springs for legs. The aliens got on all fours and did a perfect imitation of those bounding leaps, racing around in circles with the deer. And what's even weirder is I think the deer liked it. They kept coming back to jump around with the brothers from outer space.

Until one of the aliens jumped on a deer's back and tried to ride it like a rodeo cowboy. That didn't end well.

After the deer took off, a couple of raccoons showed up. Those things are pretty creepy. They crawled right into the middle of our camp, not the least bit afraid of human or alien. The raccoons sat back on their haunches and stared at us, calmly making a hand-washing gesture with their front paws, like they were showing off their opposable thumbs. Zardolph introduced himself, but the raccoons hissed and swiped at him with their claws. The alien jumped up in surprise and smacked his head on a tree branch while his brothers laughed. They spent the rest of the time climbing trees, chasing squirrels along branches, and trying to catch woodpeckers.

After camp was set up, we sat around on fallen trees and I tried to have a conversation with the Jungle Boys. You'd think this would be pretty fascinating; after all, with three aliens to talk to, you might be able to figure out some of the mysteries of the cosmos or whatever. But our conversation went something like this:

ME: So . . . how is Earth different from your home planet?
ALIEN #1: There's nobody like us here.
ALIEN #2: Yeah. And our house isn't here or anything.
ALIEN #3: I'm hungry. Mom lets us eat whatever we want on vacation. When are we going to eat?
ALIEN #2: What's that? [points at a rabbit]
ALIEN #3: Let's chase it!
ALIENS #1, 2, AND 3: Yeah! [all of them race into the bushes]

They were just too young, I guess. I shouldn't be too hard on them. If a kindergartner transported to another galaxy, he wouldn't be too great at answering a bunch of alien questions about Earth, either.

By early evening I got so hungry, I actually considered the tofu dogs in the cooler. If they were going to be halfway edible, I needed to build a fire. And to be honest, I wanted a fire for other reasons. It was going to be nighttime in a few hours, and I was a little nervous about being out here in the dark. The wild animals that had stopped by our camp all afternoon were sort of freaking me out. Not by themselves, of course. But I've seen enough Discovery Channel to know that in a place deer and rabbits called home, there also lived things that liked to eat them. Like coyotes. And bears. I figured a nice bright fire would discourage any wild beasts with sharp teeth from visiting.

The first thing to do was build a fire pit and put a circle

of rocks around it to contain the flames. I remembered reading about that trick in a book about a boy who got lost in
the wilderness with nothing but a hatchet. My plan was to
pull the wagon back to the banks of the Nooksack and fill
it with river stones. But the aliens couldn't come with me.
What if we ran into Tate and his Scouts again? One close call
was plenty. Besides, it would only take a couple of minutes.

I figured the best way to get them to behave was to keep
them busy. "Okay, guys, you see these sticks lying around?"
I picked up a fallen branch from the forest floor. "We need a
bunch of these in order to make a fire. They need to be about
this size, and you can find them right around our campsite
here. I need you all to help collect them, okay?"

They stopped chasing each other around a rotting cedar
stump. "Is it like a contest?" one of them asked.

Great idea. Even though I'd seen Tyler and his brothers
fighting all the time back home, I had forgotten the magic of
sibling rivalry, which apparently extends beyond the Earth's
atmosphere. "It sure is. Whoever can make the biggest pile
before I get back is the winner, okay?" As I left with the
wagon, they were scampering around the campsite, grabbing
sticks. "Remember, stay right around here until I get back,"
I called over my shoulder.

It took less than five minutes to walk down to the riverbank. I filled the wagon with river stones and was lugging
it back to the trail when I heard something both wonderful
and terrible.

"Hey! Scrub!"

I turned. Amy was walking toward me from upriver, picking her way across the rocks and driftwood in bare feet.

Adrenaline flooded my body. Again. I remembered my health teacher explaining that adrenaline is a powerful drug, and I wondered how many doses my heart could take in one day before it short-circuited.

I tried very hard not to look in the direction of my alien campsite, which would draw Amy's attention up there. And then I tried very hard not to spin around in circles, anxiously searching for Sheriff Tate, who could step out from behind any one of a thousand trees, holding a daughter-protecting rifle. I took a deep breath and concentrated on calmly looking at Amy. Trying to appear even semi-cool is harder than it seems.

"Hey," I said, my nerves making the word squeak out. "Why—I mean, what are—you know? How did you get, um . . . here?" I guess that even semi-coolness is beyond my reach.

Amy got closer, balancing carefully as she walked along a fallen tree. "My dad."

"Your dad?"

"Yeah. He's a troop leader, and every summer he takes his Scouts out here camping. Tonight's the big night. That's why he was looking for me when he found us at the park." She was right in front of me now, holding a little plastic bucket half filled with some kind of berries. Her legs were really tan, and her toenails were painted pink. I tried not to stare. "I stay out of their way and do my own thing. Which is fine with me. I grew up in these woods."

"Your dad." I said it flatly this time. An accusation. "You mean your dad the sheriff, the one who wants to close my grandma's place down and probably put me in jail?"

"I'm so sorry, Scrub." Amy pulled at the fraying ends of

her denim cutoff shorts. "He's not always that bad, I promise. He just takes his job way too seriously sometimes. It's been like that ever since my mom moved to California."

We were quiet then, the sounds of the river filling up the silence between us. As usual, I had no idea how to act when someone said something upsetting. Words of consolation? An apology? Questions about what happened? I had no clue, so I just stood there.

I was relieved when Amy started talking again, especially since she changed the subject, even though I know it was lame of me to feel that way.

"But what are you doing all the way out here?" she said, looking at my wagon full of rocks.

Yikes. Maybe her changing the subject wasn't such a good idea. Even if I were a great liar, it would be hard to think up a story that would explain this. I decided to stick as close to the truth as possible.

"Oh . . . just, you know . . . getting some rocks together to make a fire pit."

"I wouldn't do that if I were you. If you heat up river rocks, they'll explode."

"Really?" I studied her face, watching for the smirk. I didn't want to blindly walk into another one of her jokes.

"Really." She seemed serious enough. "Water seeps into the cracks, and then when it gets hot enough it expands and shatters the rock. What's the matter, haven't you ever read *So You Think You Can Camp?*"

I just sighed and rolled my eyes at that. "I'll have to pick up a copy."

"So you're camping out here?"

"Yeah."

"Cool! I was worried about when we might have the chance to hang out again, with my dad being so weird, but this is perfect. The swimming hole is really close to here. Want to come with me?"

It was almost impossible not to look up in the direction of the campsite. "Um . . . I don't know if that's such a good idea."

"Why not?"

"Well, your dad, you know? What if he finds us and—"

"When my dad is with his Scouts, nothing distracts him. They'll be chopping firewood and tying knots and scribbling in their nature journals until way after dark."

"Well . . . what if he comes to check on you?"

"Nah. He lets me do my own thing. My tent is pretty close, but it isn't technically at their same campsite, to make sure I don't mess up their male-bonding time or whatever." She reached out and took me by the hand. Just like that. "Come on, at least pick some berries with me," she said.

I snuck a look up in the direction of my campsite. All clear. Then I looked back at Amy. I noticed for the first time that her eyes were two different colors, one greenish and one brownish. Very cool. Amy stood between me and the river, and when the late evening sun glinted off the surface of the water, it almost looked like she was glowing.

Amy's hand was warm against mine. She gave it a small tug, pulling me upriver. "The red huckleberry bush is right over here."

I exhaled, relieved. I could still watch the campsite—or at least keep an eye out in that direction—while we stood at her berry bush. I could spare a couple of minutes. "Sounds good. But what are huckleberries?"

"You've never had a huckleberry? Here, try one." Amy plucked a berry, small and pink and perfectly round, and put it in my mouth. It was really good, kind of tart and sweet at the same time.

It took us a little while to fill up the bucket, partly because the berries were so small, but mostly because we ate two or three for every one that we dropped in. I tried to keep an eye on the hill, in the direction of the Jungle Boys, but to be honest, it was pretty easy to forget about the aliens for a few minutes because Amy and I were talking the whole time.

And this time I wasn't really nervous about talking with a girl. Maybe because we had broken the ice earlier at the park, but it was just like talking to a normal person. Okay, of course I realized she's a *normal* person. It's just that it was really fun and easy to talk with her, like talking to a friend or something. Maybe she was my friend. Whatever.

Anyway, it was nice to know we had so much in common. I thought it might be hard to keep a conversation going with someone who lived 3,000 miles away, but with the Internet and TV and stuff, it turned out we had a lot of the same interests. She even liked to play video games, which was cool, because not many of the girls I know are interested in gaming. Then we started talking about our favorite bands, and I learned that she had taken guitar lessons for over three years.

"You really play guitar?" I asked.

"Yeah. I've been practicing on an old acoustic I found at a garage sale. But I've been hinting that I want an electric

Fender for my birthday next month." She munched on a few huckleberries. "Actually, I guess *hinting* isn't really the right word. More like *begging*. But sometimes my dad is pretty clueless when it comes to good presents. So I figured I'd give him a little help."

At the mention of her dad I started thinking I should get back to camp. A breeze caused a rash of goose bumps to raise up on my forearm, and I realized the temperature had dropped. Dusk was coming on fast.

"Hey, Amy, I think I better get going," I said.

"Are you sure?"

"Yeah. I need to get back to my campsite before it gets dark. I want to make sure I can still find it, you know?"

"Do you want me to walk you back?"

"No!" I must have said it a little too eagerly, or maybe even yelled it, because she looked kind of taken aback. "I mean, that's a really nice offer. And I had a great time today. Really. But . . . I think I better walk back by myself."

"Why's that?"

"Oh, um, . . . it's . . . just part of this dare that I have with a friend back home. He challenged me to camp all by myself for a night in the woods. Doesn't think I can do it. If you were there, even for a few minutes, it might sort of be cheating, you know?"

I think it worked, because she smiled at me again. Maybe I was starting to get the hang of talking to girls. Even if I had to fib to keep her away from Campsite Area 51.

"So you're camping out here all by yourself?" she asked.

"Yeah."

"Wow. That's pretty brave," she said. I smiled. I couldn't help it. No one had ever called me brave before. "Especially with all the bears around here," she added.

"Bears?" I scanned the forest furtively, as if a giant grizzly was about to attack. My face must have looked as terrified as I felt, because she laughed.

"Nah, I'm just playing. I've never seen a bear out here." She sat on a rock and pulled a sweatshirt over her head. "If you get lonely up there, you can come find my campsite. It's just up the trail. I'm a pretty good fire builder, and I stole a big bag of marshmallows from the Scout supplies." She took hold of my hand again. "That wouldn't be cheating on your dare, would it?"

"Nah. That sounds good," I said. I knew I wouldn't be able to visit her, but it was nice that she asked me.

"Just make sure my dad doesn't see you."

"Good idea. See ya." I squeezed her hand, and she squeezed back. I walked to my wagon and pulled it up the hill toward the campsite. For some reason, it seemed a lot lighter.

But probably just because I'd dumped out all the river stones.

10

I couldn't believe how much darker it was in the middle of the trees than in the clearing by the water, where I could still see the sky. I tripped over tree roots a couple of times and fell facedown on the forest floor, and when I stood up there were leaves and twigs stuck in my hair and hanging down into my eyes.

The sky stayed light until almost ten o'clock in town. It was only nine now, but so dark in the forest, I nearly ran right into the tent before I figured out where I was. When my eyes finally adjusted to the lack of light, I saw there was no need to worry about the aliens. Around the edges of the campsite were three enormous piles of wood. No, these were *towers* of wood, each one easily over twenty feet tall and as wide at the base as the floor of my bedroom. Man, they were fast; I could only have been gone for fifteen minutes, maybe twenty. (Okay, so maybe it was longer and I kind of lost track of time with Amy. But whatever—I was back and they were still here and that's all that mattered.)

At the bottom of each firewood tower was an alien, sprawled out on the ground and breathing heavily. I guess there was a limit to their extraterrestrial supply of energy after all. They slowly lifted their heads off the ground for a moment to look at me, but then plopped back down on the forest floor.

"We tried to keep working," one of them wheezed. "But there are no more stick things around here." I believed it. From what I could see of the surrounding forest floor, it looked like it had been gone over with a vacuum cleaner.

One alien managed to push himself into a sitting position, his palm fronds drooping down over his face. "Do you think we got enough sticks for the fire?"

I craned my neck, but the tops of the towers were lost in the deepening blackness. "Yeah, I think that will be fine, guys. Good work." I rummaged through the supplies in the wagon, squinting to find a flashlight. When I finally grabbed one and switched it on, the tiny lightbulb flared briefly... then flickered and died.

I tried hitting it a few times with the palm of my hand.

I wonder if that has *ever* worked. "Great," I muttered. "No light. How am I supposed to build a fire in total darkness?"

I shoved my hands into the duffel bag, blindly scrounging for a second flashlight I knew wasn't there, when suddenly the entire campsite was lit up by a greenish glow. Sometimes, in movies, the camera shows what it looks like when some military guy is looking through night-vision goggles. You know it's supposed to be dark, but you can still see everything, and it all looks kind of green. It was like that. Only brighter, maybe.

"Does this help?" said Zardolph. I turned, and he was glowing all over. Well, I guess not all over, but those green and yellow blotches that covered his body were shining pretty intensely. Zardolph stood up and spread his arms and legs out, and the campsite got even brighter.

"Wow. How do you do that?" I asked.

"Easy. I just do it," he said. "I was wondering why *you* weren't doing it when you said you needed light. Earthlings are weird."

I smiled. It had been a long day, but at least I had gotten to see Amy again, and the three aliens under my supervision were all accounted for, relatively safe, and undetected by the citizens of Earth. "Yeah, I guess we are kind of weird," I said. I felt pretty tired all of a sudden. Digging a pit and getting a fire going didn't sound too appealing. I looked over to where the other two aliens were sprawled out on the forest floor. "Are your brothers asleep?" I asked.

"Yes. Traveling kind of wears them out."

"Are you hungry?"

"No. We ate the bars named Hershey from your box. Delicious."

Great. Cold tofu dogs for my dinner. "Can you help me get these two into the tent? I think we'll call it a night."

A couple of hours later the aliens were sleeping soundly, while I stared at the ceiling of the tent. I checked the glowing readout on my watch. 11:17. Sometimes I can't shut my brain off at night, and it's hard to get to sleep. I closed my eyes and tried to think about nothing, but my mind kept offering things to think about anyway. It shouldn't have surprised me that most of those things had to do with Amy.

I remembered everything I had said to her. Only now, in the calm of the tent and with lots of time to think, I came up with way cooler things I could have said. I wished I had a time machine so I could go back and erase my doofus mistakes. Who knows? I guess if someone could invent an intergalactic transporter, then maybe someone could come up with a time machine.

I tried to imagine what Amy was doing at that moment. Was she asleep, or sitting up by the campfire? Maybe she'd snuck up on the Scouts' tents and was listening to them tell ghost stories. I tried to picture her reaction if I were to show up at her campsite. Surprised? Happy, maybe? It's hard to tell with girls. Most of the stuff I think about them ends up being wrong. But I couldn't shake the feeling she might be a little bit happy if I showed up over there. Just for a few minutes. A quick hello, then come right back.

I craned my neck and looked over at the aliens. Still

sleeping. I stretched out my arm and shook one of them. The green and yellow splotches flared up brightly for a second, then faded. He slept right through it.

I got on all fours, unzipped the entryway as quietly as I could, then crawled out of the tent. I didn't feel nervous about leaving the aliens this time. They were clearly exhausted from all of their running around the entire day. I could easily pop over for a minute and then come right back. The aliens would never even know I was gone.

Walking through the forest without a flashlight wasn't as scary as I thought it would be. The moon was bright now, and small clearings in the canopy of branches overhead let a little light through. The moonlight turned the pine needles silver, and I wasn't too worried about running into a tree or a thorny blackberry bramble. I realized that I must really like Amy if I was out here with all of those wild animals that called the forest home; I just prayed they would stay in their nice warm beds tonight.

I walked toward the sound of rushing water, and when I reached the river I followed it downstream. Pretty soon I saw the flicker of a campfire through the trees.

I crept up until I could see the campsite. I was worried about running across Tate and the Scouts first, but their site must have been farther down the trail. There was Amy, sitting on a log by the campfire, strumming a guitar and singing. I edged closer until I was behind a tree right next to her clearing. I recognized the tune of her song from the radio, but I don't listen to country stations that much, so I didn't know the words or who sang it or anything. She was strumming for most of the song, but when she got to the chorus—something about dancing—she did this quick fingerpicking thing where she plucked out individual notes. She was really, really good.

It was nice just to stand there and watch her. The forest behind Amy was black, and the fire lit her up against it, like a spotlight on a stage.

When she finished her song, I applauded and stepped out from behind the tree. She looked scared for a second, and I was afraid that maybe she was mad that I had come over, but then she smiled.

"Scrub! You startled me!"

"Sorry," I whispered, and took a few steps into the clearing. "How's it going? Have the Scouts come over to freak you out or anything like that?" I tried to see beyond the clearing, but the fire had ruined my night vision. Everything was pitch-black.

"Nah, they're under strict orders from Dad to leave me alone. I won't see them until breakfast."

I nodded. And stood there. Then nodded and stood there some more. I guess I should have made more of a plan about what I would do when I actually made it over here. Thankfully, Amy broke the silence.

"So how's your solo camping night going?" she asked.

"Oh, yeah... it's good. Fine." Amy continued to look at me. Finally the fog cleared and I came up with the brilliant idea to give her a compliment. "You're a really good guitar player."

Amy's cheeks turned a bit more red in the glow of the campfire, and she looked at her guitar. "Not really. But it's fun." She strummed a few times. "Do you play?"

"Me? No way. I'm not musical at all." Which is true. In fifth-grade band I was so bad at playing the bass drum that

I messed up everyone's timing and Mr. Perry made me his teacher's assistant instead.

"Come here, I'll show you." I started to protest, but Amy patted the log, inviting me to sit down beside her, and I realized maybe it wasn't such a bad idea after all.

I sat on the fallen tree, a patch of moss providing a cushion, and Amy set the guitar on my lap. It seemed way bigger up close like this. "Here, I'll teach you how to play a 'G.' It's my favorite chord." She wrapped her warm fingers around my left wrist and positioned it high on the neck of the guitar. Then she gently stretched my fingers apart and placed them all on different strings. "Okay, now press down."

"This feels really weird."

She nodded. "Doesn't it? The first time you learn how to finger a chord it seems impossible. But after a while it becomes second nature."

"Am I doing it right?"

"The sound test will decide." She slipped a pick between the thumb and forefinger of my right hand. "Give it a strum."

I let the pick fall across all six strings. There was a buzzing noise, but that was drowned out by a harsh twang that made me wince.

Amy laughed, and I instantly felt my face flashing hot. But when I looked from the guitar to her face, Amy's eyes were full of her smile, and it was easy to tell she wasn't laughing at me in a mean way.

"So, 'G' is your favorite chord, huh?" I said. "I don't know why. It sounds pretty hideous to me." She laughed again, louder, and this time it felt great.

"I think I messed up the fingering. It's backwards with me

facing the guitar," she said. "Here, I think this will help." She stood and moved behind me, then leaned over my shoulder and rearranged my fingers. "The buzzing sound is because your fingers need to be between the frets—these little lines here—not on top of them," she said. Her hair brushed against my neck, and I wondered if she could actually hear my heartbeat. "And the hideous part is because these two fingers are out of position. So you're way out of tune." She leaned over farther to correct the problem. She was sort of pressed against my back, and now I wondered if she could *feel* my racing heartbeat. "Try it again."

I strummed. It was perfect, a deep note with a light finish.

Amy sat on the log and applauded. "A very nice 'G.' Especially for a beginner."

I strummed a few more times, bobbing my head with my eyes closed like I really knew what I was doing, a blues musician lost in a musical trance. More laughter and applause from Amy.

"Thanks," I said. Then I put the guitar on the ground, and it was just us. No aliens, no sheriff, no Grandma. Just us and the log and the campfire.

We did some talking then, but I have to be honest, I don't remember one word. Because all I could think about was how if there was ever an opportunity for me to kiss a girl, this was it.

It's weird to talk to someone that you might try to kiss. Really weird. Because all I could do was stare at her lips. It was very hard to comprehend the words coming out of her mouth, because all I could think about was what it would feel like for that mouth to be sort of smooshed up against mine.

And after a while I got even more flustered, because I thought that maybe, just maybe, she was looking at my lips, too . . . and then it seemed like my lips didn't work right anymore. It's hard to explain, but when I thought she might be looking at my lips, I started to worry about what they looked like, which I had never done before, and then they felt kind of numb.

Even though I hadn't followed our conversation too closely, I realized that it had definitely stopped. And then our faces were moving closer to each other, even though it didn't feel like I was consciously moving my head at all.

I had a moment to realize that I had no idea how to kiss someone, and then another moment to realize that I didn't care too much, and then I remembered that you're supposed to close your eyes.

And then we were kissing. Her lips were soft and warm, and they tasted a little bit like huckleberries.

19

I half opened my eyes in mid-kiss. Not sure why. Everything felt so perfect, maybe I wanted to make sure it was real.

You always hear that people see fireworks during a great first kiss, big explosions of color and light and all of that. But for me it was a soft, greenish glow, dancing just on the outside of my field of vision. I closed my eyes again and kissed a little more.

My eyes flew wide open. Greenish glow?

There! A Jungle Boy, running through the dark forest!

And behind him, two more, disappearing behind a wall of trees.

My heart redlined. I didn't want to leave Amy, but I had to go. No time to stay and explain. How would I explain, anyway?

I must have stopped kissing, because Amy pulled back, eyes open. "Are you okay?" she asked. "You look kind of . . . scared."

My body wanted to race into the forest, but I forced myself back into the moment. I didn't want to screw this up now. "I'm fine," I said. "Really. That was amazing."

She blushed, and lowered her eyes. "Yeah."

"And now I have to go."

"Are you sure?" she said.

"Yes. And I'm sorry. But I'll talk to you again soon, okay?"

She looked like she was about to say something, but instead she just nodded. I reached out, found her hand, and squeezed. She squeezed back.

And then I was off, crashing through the ferns and into the black forest. Panic quickly crowded all other emotions out of my adrenaline-soaked brain.

I ran through the woods with both hands in front of my face to ward off the branches that threatened to clothesline me or poke an eye out. I tripped and fell into a patch of stinging nettles that set my arms on fire. Thorny bushes ripped at my clothes, and I was bleeding from at least a few different places.

What a frustrating chase. Again and again I closed in on a bobbing green glow, only to have it disappear behind a tree or around a bend in the river. The aliens were really moving fast, but at least they seemed to be sticking pretty close to the water. If they turned and went up into the foothills and mountains and hundreds of miles of uninterrupted forest, there's no telling what might happen to them. Or to me.

But when I fought my way through a thicket of undergrowth and saw the three aliens standing on top of a rocky ridge, I realized things could get much worse than being hopelessly lost in the untamed wilderness. Because at the bottom of the ridge was a circle of Scouts sitting around a campfire. And there was troop leader Tate, standing by a group of pup tents. And all of them were staring up at the glowing visitors from outer space.

20

For a stomach-churning moment the aliens and the humans just stood there, staring at each other.

So eerily still were the Jungle Boys that it was hard to tell which group was more surprised to find the other out here in the middle of the forest. The aliens stood and stared, their glowing blotches pulsating now in the rhythm of a blinking traffic light. It was impossible to make out their bodies or faces against the black backdrop of night; they just looked like eerie splotches of glowing color. And since the ridge was probably fifteen feet high, it looked like the colors were floating in midair.

The young Scouts stared back, each mouth forming a surprised circle, their marshmallows dropping from the end of forgotten skewers right into the middle of the fire.

I was as still as everyone else. It probably only lasted four or five seconds at most, but it was like watching my worst nightmare come true on a giant movie screen, and I could only stare, unable to do anything about it.

Then the aliens switched off their glow and disappeared from sight. The Scouts found their voices.

"Did you see that?"

"What was it?"

"There was more than one."

"I bet it was Eddie and the older kids playing a joke."

"Yeah, with flashlights or something. Had to be."

"No way! We're right here!"

"Then what was—"

"Silence!" Tate roared. "All of you! Still and quiet. Now!"

A hush fell over the campsite, the Scouts straining their eyes and ears into the night. Tate took a couple of slow, backward steps toward one of the tents, his eyes still fixed in the direction of the ridge.

I crept closer to the campsite, trying not to step on a twig or rustle any bushes. I was only worried about noise, as the Scouts wouldn't be able to see past the light cast by the campfire. I knew from being over at Amy's that it was like looking into a house at night—the person on the outside could see into the house perfectly, but whoever was inside the house couldn't see past the window.

At the bottom of the ridge I craned my head to look up and could just make out the outlines of the aliens' dark bodies, and I waved my hands over my head to get their attention.

They didn't see me. One of them bent over and picked something off the rock. He straightened up, then hurled it toward the group of Scouts. He used the exact motion that I had taught him while skipping rocks at the river earlier that day.

Thunk! A pinecone bounced off the head of one of the Scouts. I squinted and could just make out that it was Eddie, staring vacantly up at the ridge. The aliens pointed their tendrils at him, chittering away in high-pitched laughter.

That stirred up the action at the campsite, like poking a stick into a quiet wasps' nest, and the whole place burst into activity. The circle of Scouts broke, some of them sprinting for the safety of the tents, others running aimlessly around the campsite, yelling, and the rest picking up pinecones to fire back up at the ridge.

The Jungle Boys found this a great game. They leaped down from the top of the ridge and ran circles around the campsite, periodically switching on their body lights to create a vague greenish-yellow blur around the perimeter. Then they took to the surrounding trees, scrambling up trunks and sliding along branches, dodging the Scouts' wildly inaccurate pinecone tosses and laughing the whole time.

Sheriff Tate barked out a series of orders that no one followed, or even seemed to hear. "Stay near the fire! Stop running around and get into one big group! Beware of those lights, they might be dangerous!" He punctuated each unheeded order by pointing to various places around the campsite and clapping his hands to try and get someone's —anyone's—attention.

I got dizzy watching the blur of activity before me. There was so much to see, and it all happened so fast that I didn't even know how I was feeling yet. I was totally numb; not just my body, but my brain, too.

Then I saw two things that broke the paralysis. The first was a pudgy boy with a blond crew cut sitting by the fire. He clutched a cell phone in both hands, snapping pictures of the scene before him, the little flash lighting up the night. The second thing was Sheriff Tate, ducking into one of the tents and coming out holding that hunting rifle.

Only one thing would be worse than alien photos making it back to civilization: dead-alien photos doing the same thing. Time to act.

I ran around the perimeter of the campsite, careful to stay out of the ring of light projected by the campfire. I tried to head off one of the aliens, who was racing around from the other direction on all fours. I reached out for him, but he spun away from my outstretched arms and dashed right by me, chittering away the whole time.

I turned and ran back the way I had come. The shouts from the camp were getting closer. I had to do something fast. Another alien came barreling toward me. When he got close, I went into point-guard mode, faking a step left and then moving quickly to the right. The alien fell for it. We smashed together and rolled into a clump of fern bushes.

He tried to wriggle away, but I caught him in a bear hug

and didn't let go, even though the collision had knocked the wind out of me. The alien tried to break free of my grip, his tubular torso slithering between my arms. I finally managed to climb up on all fours and pin him down with my knees, desperately trying to suck in some air.

"What are you doing?" I croaked.

"Playing with the earthlings. They are a lot more fun than the forest beasts."

"You have to stop! We're going to get in big trouble!"

"Trouble?" The alien stopped trying to snake his way out from under me. His body went still and his eyes grew round with fright, just like an earthling's. "You won't tell our parents, will you?"

"Not if you help me get out of here. Now!" I looked over at the campsite. It was still chaos, but I could see some of the Scouts inching their way over to us. I knew they couldn't see us, but I'm sure they could track the thrashing sound from the bushes.

"What do you want me to do?" the alien whispered.

"Get your brothers over here. Quick!" I rolled off the alien, and he sprang to his feet. He leaned forward and made a screeching sound by rubbing his antennae together rapidly. His brothers stopped circling the campsite and ran straight to us.

"Turn off your lights! All of you!" I whispered. The aliens instantly went dark. The Scouts stood staring, blinking, into the dark forest.

Then I heard Sheriff Tate shout, "Get on the ground, boys. Now!" The Scouts flopped onto the forest floor.

Tate hefted the rifle up to his shoulder and pointed it into the blackness. I swung my arm around the aliens' shoulders and pulled them to their knees into a tight huddle.

Blam! The air split near my cheek as a bullet whistled by. A patch of bark on the tree behind us exploded.

I grabbed as many arms as I could and pulled the aliens into the dark forest. "Run!" I yelled, although I didn't need to. The Jungle Boys had gotten the idea.

We blundered through the underbrush, branches clawing at my face and body. The gun exploded two more times.

The four of us stumbled onto the riverside trail. I wondered if we had enough time to find a hiding place or maybe climb a tree. But the aliens didn't slow down; instead of following the trail they headed straight, across the stones and over the river, flapping their tendrils on top of the white water and out of sight.

I hesitated for a second and then followed, charging into the river. The cold took my breath away. The water was only mid-thigh deep, but as soon as I tried to wade across, my foot hit a slimy rock and I fell face-first, my entire body plunging below the surface. The current caught me and spun me around, and I did two sideways somersaults as the water dragged me downriver, before I regained my footing. I stood up, choking and retching, and blindly took a few steps. I had gotten twisted around and was now wading back toward the original bank.

And there was Sheriff Tate, running along the edge of the river, coming right for me. I stopped, the current pulling at my freezing legs, and stared back. He pointed right at me. "You!" he yelled, the moonlight catching his face and making him look ghoulish.

I turned and waded away, but my feet slid across the slick stones underneath the water, and the current sucked me in again. It was a struggle just to stay upright, let alone make it to the other shore. I squinted through the darkness and could just make out the other side. It seemed an impossible distance.

I heard Tate splash into the river behind me. "You!" he yelled again, and he sounded much closer.

I fell to my knees and tried to crawl away, but the water splashed up into my face, blinding me. The current pulled me underneath yet again. My knee banged into a submerged boulder, and the pain exploded all up and down my leg. I tried to grab the huge rock to steady myself, but it was slimy, too, and I slid right off.

I stopped fighting and surrendered myself to the will of the river. It dragged and tossed me like a fallen leaf. I didn't even care about getting to the other side anymore; I just needed to get my head above water for a breath of air.

Suddenly I was jerked out of the water. I thought it was the sheriff, but then I realized there were too many hands.

The Jungle Boys hoisted me in the air and ran along the surface of the river to the other side. Then everything went black.

21

I woke up in my bed at Grandma's place, still wearing muddy jeans and a ripped-up flannel shirt. Daylight filled the room. How late was it?

I rolled out of bed, wincing at the soreness in my knee and dozens of cuts and bruises all over. Ignoring the pain, I trudged toward the door. I had to find out how bad things were.

It didn't take long. Just outside my door a crowd of customers rushed about, getting in each other's way and spilling clothes from half-open suitcases.

Grandma was in the middle of it all, directing traffic. Her face was emotionless, all business.

"The transporter in that room has stopped working. It's seen some heavy use this morning," she said to a group of furry Tourists. She ushered them into the room next to mine. "This one should work for you, but there's a bit of a line. You'll have to wait a few moments." She untangled three aliens who had run straight into each other and now sat in the middle of the hall in a heap.

"I can't believe we're being forced to leave so early," one of them snarled as he struggled to get to his feet. "I'm never coming back here again."

"My apologies, sir." It came out flat, with none of her usual warmth or concern. The alien glared at her, but she already had her back turned to him as she walked away to help some others carry their suitcases into one of the rooms.

I stood in the middle of it all, feeling numb, the Tourists knocking into me as they rushed past. No one was worried about disguises this morning, so the hallway looked like happy hour at that saloon in *Star Wars*. Grandma emerged from one of the bedrooms and our eyes met. She looked exhausted, and it was the only time I had ever seen her without a smile in her eyes.

"How bad?" I asked.

She pointed at a copy of *The Forest Grove Gazette* lying on a chair. "Read that," she said in that same flat, tired tone. "Then meet me downstairs." She rushed past me and hurried down the steps. I stepped back into my room and looked at the big headline splashed across the front page:

ALIEN SIGHTING IN FOREST GROVE: FACT OR FICTION?

My stomach knotted up and I thought I was going to puke. Oh, man, this was so much worse than the thing at the park with Mr. Harnox and the teenagers. This was...this was the worst thing I could ever have let happen.

Underneath the headline: a picture of one of the Jungle Boys, the glow from his body lighting up the forest behind him. It was like those famous pictures of the Loch Ness Monster or Bigfoot. Grainy. Out of focus. Obviously amateurish, or in this case, taken by a cheap cell phone.

But also like with those famous photographs, your imagination became the camera. It smoothed out the blurry edges. Added depth to a flat image. Found features and details in confused shadows. And then, because some part of your mind *wanted* to believe, it would let you see a clear picture of a mythical beast.

Or, in this case, you saw exactly what was there: a picture of a glowing alien, obscured by some leafy maple branches, throwing pinecones in the forest.

I scanned the article:

FOREST GROVE—Robert Tate, Forest Grove's sheriff for nearly two decades, claims he encountered extraterrestrial life forms in the forest north of town late last night.

Tate, also the leader of Cub Scout Troop #17, was camping with a dozen Scouts near the Nooksack River when the mysterious event allegedly occurred just before midnight. As proof, he offers a picture taken by one of the Scouts (see photo above).

"There was a pack of them, maybe ten in all. Their bodies were all lit up and they had the ability to fly," Tate said. "They were extremely hostile and launched an attack on our campsite. My first priority, as always, was protecting my Scouts."

The sheriff said he plans to rally community support against The Intergalactic Bed and Breakfast, a local establishment that caters to (story continued on page A7)

I tossed the newspaper aside and rush-limped down the staircase, the hallways empty now. Mr. Harnox was alone in the sitting room, crouching at one of the windows and peeking outside from behind the edge of a curtain. All of the windows were covered.

I pushed aside a corner of the curtain on the next window and looked out. The sight knocked the wind out of me.

Hundreds of people were gathered out front, pressed up against the white picket fence and lining the sidewalks. Some looked through binoculars, and others fiddled with video cameras, apparently preparing for a mob of hostile aliens to run out the front door at any moment.

And there, off to the side of the front porch, a dozen or so men circled Sheriff Tate as he spoke into a walkie-talkie. Most of them were holding shotguns or hunting rifles.

I heard a creak on the stairs. I dropped the curtain and saw Grandma making her way down, holding the railing for support.

"I managed to get the rest of the Tourists out safely," she

said. There were dark circles under her eyes, and for the first time since I'd met her, she looked old. She also looked miserable, but nowhere close to as bad as I felt for causing her to look that way.

"What about the three alien boys?" I asked.

"Their parents got here at the crack of dawn and picked them up. They're safe."

"Grandma, I'm so sorry. I didn't—"

Grandma stepped close and put a finger on my lips. "Shhh. First things first. Are you all right?"

"I'm fine, but—"

"You're well and truly all right, then. You promise?" she asked. She felt my forehead, then studied me. "You were so feverish when they brought you home last night. Delirious. Oh, was I worried. Thank the Creator you're okay." She let out a long, shaky breath. "I stayed with you all night, but before you awoke, *they* showed up outside, and then... then..." She trailed off, too upset to continue.

I put my arm around her shoulders and led her away from the window. I tried to set her down on the couch but she shook me off. "Scrub, there's something we need to talk about."

I nodded a little, too nervous to speak.

"When those giant Tourists came to collect their children...we asked the boys for their version of what had happened...."

I swallowed. I felt like running from the room, hiding somewhere. I knew Grandma wanted me to say something, but I wasn't strong enough.

"They told us..." She took a deep breath. "Scrub, they

told us that you left them alone in the forest. In the middle of the night. All three of them said they went out looking for you, and that's when they ran into Tate and the Scouts." She studied my face, waiting for a reaction. I could feel the hot pinpricks of tears behind my eyes, but I refused to let them fall.

Grandma kept her gaze fixed on my face. "I stood up for you. Told the parents that simply couldn't be true, that you would never do something like that."

I wanted so badly to deny everything. The perfect lie even popped into my head: I had stepped out around midnight to go to the bathroom behind some nearby trees when the Jungle Boys popped out of the tent and ran away... they had been so mischievous all day... they were probably just *waiting* for me to drop my guard for a split second so they could escape and cause trouble... I could see it all so clearly that I even started to believe it for a minute.

Grandma was watching me carefully, a glimmer of hope in her eyes. I could tell she would believe anything I said right then.

I opened my mouth, but the story refused to come out. Grandma had trusted me so much since I got here, the only adult who had ever really trusted me with anything, and I couldn't pay that back with a lie.

I stared at the floor. "It's true," I said. I heard Grandma let out a little gasp. I kept looking at the floor for a minute, but then forced myself to look up, into her eyes. "They were sleeping so hard. I figured I could sneak away, just for a few minutes. I thought everything would be fine."

If Grandma had yelled at me, I think I could have handled it. But it was so much worse when tears leaked out from behind her pink lenses and she looked right through me. "Oh, Scrub. How could you?" She turned to fix her glazed-over stare at the curtains. "And now Tate has won. The whole town's out there. I'm ruined." She slumped down on the couch, any traces of her normal energy gone. She looked like a puppet with all of the strings cut.

I knelt beside her. "Grandma, I am so sorry, I can—"

She held up a hand to cut me off. "No. No. It's mostly my fault," she said, not even looking at me, her voice barely audible. "I never should have asked you to go. It was just too much responsibility to burden you with. I realize that now."

"No! That's not true, Grandma. I can handle it, I promise. I *like* the responsibility." She stared at her hands, which were lying palms up on her lap. "If you give me a second chance, I swear I'll never let you down again."

"I wish I could give you that chance, Scrub, and never were words more true." Grandma sighed. "But those people outside have invited fear into their hearts, and now fear has made its home there." She dabbed at the corners of her eyes behind her glasses, then gestured toward the window with one skinny arm. "Just look at them. The fear twists their faces so badly that they need some of our disguises just to look like themselves again. I'm afraid they won't allow me the opportunity to offer you a second chance."

The stark reality of that fact was impossible to ignore. My body felt like shutting down. I was tired, sore, furious with myself for getting into this mess and—I could admit it—afraid of the mob outside. But I had to fight against all of that; I had to keep a window of hope open, or I'd never be able to forgive myself.

"I can fix this," I told Grandma. "I can get rid of that mob and save your business."

She looked up from her hands and gazed steadily at me. "How?"

I took a deep breath. "I don't know yet."

Bam! Bam bam bam! Bam!

Grandma's head jerked up. Mr. Harnox dropped the edge of the curtain and scrambled backward. "Some of them, out there," he said, gesturing to the window. "They are throwing—"

Crash! A rock smashed through the window and lay on the carpet, surrounded by shards of glass.

I ran to another window and peeked out from behind the drapes. Sheriff Tate and a few of his men were herding a group of teenagers—Eddie and Brian among them, clutching rocks—away from the house.

"You kids get outta here!" he shouted. "This could get dangerous. It's a man's job." The teenagers took a couple of reluctant steps backward, and Tate kept shooing them. "Go on, now." He raised his voice to address the rest of the crowd. "The women, children, and elderly should clear out too. No telling what might transpire here today. Leave this to the men." A few people backed up a little bit, but most of the mob remained just as it was. Some of them shouted out at Tate, things like: "We have a right to be here!" and "We care about the safety of this town just as much as you do!"

I dropped the curtain and crossed to Grandma, who was

looking more alert now. Mr. Harnox approached us. "Excuse and pardon... but have you thought the idea... to be making some contact with the Intergalactic Police Force?"

"We can't do that!" Grandma came all the way to life again. She jumped off the couch and paced around the sitting room. "They'll shut down the transporters. Maybe forever. Even if we do somehow manage to get rid of Tate and the rest of those human fools, I'd still be out of business." She did a few more laps around the sitting room, shaking her head and muttering to herself.

She looked a little crazed. Mr. Harnox moved to put a hand on her shoulder. "But, please, it is the only way that—" he started to say, but Grandma shook him off and marched toward the front door.

"That's it. I'm going out there to give that horrible man something's he's needed for too many years."

"No!" I said. I had a vision of her on a rampage, wild-eyed, taking a swing at the sheriff in front of a crowd of angry witnesses. I didn't think it would help our cause.

I rushed to cut her off. The doorknob was in her hand, and she had pulled the door halfway open when I reached her and grabbed her in a bear hug. Mr. Harnox followed, shutting the door and helping me sit Grandma down on the couch again.

"Let's try to think this through for a minute. Okay?" I said. Grandma relaxed a bit, nodded at me. "What's the Intergalactic Police Force?"

"Oh, just what it sounds like." Grandma sighed, her face draining from an angry red to a defeated pale gray. "Made up of law enforcement types from planets across the Interplanetary Collective. They respond to situations all over the cosmos. But you're only supposed to call them in a dire emergency."

The sounds of the assembled crowd were louder now, coming in through the shattered window. "Well, Grandma...I think this is an emergency," I said.

"But I've never had to call them. Not once, in over forty years."

I winced. I didn't think I could possibly feel any worse, but the knife of guilt twisted even deeper into my belly.

A long moment passed before Grandma spoke again. "Oh, I suppose you're right, Mr. Harnox. It's our only option at this point."

Mr. Harnox nodded slowly. Grandma looked up at me then, and she seemed a little more like her old self. "According to the official protocol, I'm supposed to get in touch if there is any breach in security. But I just dread calling them. Who knows what they'll do when they see that crowd of hostile humans outside?"

"Let's worry about one thing at a time," I said. I tried to stay focused on the task at hand to keep the fear and the guilt from clouding up my mind. "How do we contact the Intergalactic Police?"

"We need to get to a transporter," she said. I pulled Grandma out of her seat and escorted her down the hall. Mr. Harnox followed.

"Then we'd better do it pretty quick," I said.

We hurried up the stairs and entered the first guest room that we came to. I tapped on the transporter door. "Now, how do we do this?"

"We need to punch in our code—it contains the ID

number for the inn, along with our planetary longitude and latitude coordinates."

I gestured to the transporter input console. "Okay, go ahead and type it in."

"It's a really long number." Grandma made a face. "I can never remember it."

"Then how—"

"Wait, I know just where to find it." Grandma stepped out and opened up a storage closet. Mr. Harnox helped her drag a bunch of rumpled cardboard boxes into the hall. Finally she found the right one and started lifting out papers. Dust clouds billowed up from the boxes and hung in the air above her.

I nudged the edge of a curtain and peeked out the window. The crowd looked bigger from up here, and it was growing by the minute. People had spilled over the fence and were filling up the lawn. The front lines were swelling dangerously close to the porch.

Mr. Harnox came and stood over my shoulder, studying the crowd. He gave me a very worried look, and I put a finger to my lips and shook my head.

"Grandma." I tried to block out the panic, keep my voice neutral. "I think we need to hurry up a little because—"

"Got it," Grandma said, hurrying back into the room. "We just enter these numbers here"—she stepped up to the console, punching buttons while she looked at the paper—"and then enter the number code for the IGPF, kind of an Outer Space nine-one-one. There." She stepped back but kept looking at the console for a moment. "They should get the message instantaneously."

Grandma shut the transporter door. The blue circle appeared briefly, then flared out. She turned and faced me and Mr. Harnox. "It's done," she said in a small voice.

"You said something about them shutting down the transporters?"

Grandma nodded. "I've heard some variation of the same story from many Tourists. Apparently the IGPF took control of the transporter system hundreds of years ago, after a mass escape from a prison planet in a remote galaxy. Once the inmates stormed through the transporters, they were impossible to find. Now the police can shut down any and all transporters remotely with the touch of a button. As soon as they get an emergency call, they turn off the transporters for that location until everything has been resolved." She put her hand on Mr. Harnox's arm. "And you've been waiting so long to go home, you poor thing. Who knows how long it will be now?"

Mr. Harnox put one of his gray hands on top of Grandma's and patted her. "It is not the problem," he said. "I would not leave while the danger was all around, in any case."

I admit, it stung a little to realize I had a lot to learn about bravery and treating others humanely from someone who lived millions of light-years from Earth.

"So what do we do now?" I said.

Grandma sighed. "We wait for them to show up."

I thought of the growing crowd outside. "When will that be?"

"Hopefully, soon." She leaned in and whispered to me. "At the very least they can protect Mr. Harnox. There's no telling what Tate and that crowd would do if they got their hands on him in the middle of their frenzy."

I shuddered at the thought. "What can I do to help?" I asked. "There must be something."

Grandma chewed her bottom lip for a minute. "We need to keep Tate and that crowd out of this house until they get here."

A booming knock on the front door. We all jumped. "I'll get it," I said. I was terrified about what I would find on the other side of that door, but it felt good to be doing *something*, to at least work some of the adrenaline out of my body.

We trotted down the stairs and opened the door, and there was Tate in his sheriff's uniform. Standing behind him on the porch was Deputy Tisdall, along with a few of those men with guns. Tate wore the sunglasses that obscured his eyes and chomped on another one of his toothpicks. Most horribly, he was smiling.

"Pardon me, ma'am," he said. "But the citizens of this town will no longer stand for your shenanigans, especially when they put others in danger." Here he gestured to the mob behind him.

Grandma just stared at him, speechless. It was disturbing to see her look helpless in front of him.

"I have a petition signed by several good people from town," Tate said, waving a clipboard in Grandma's face. "It calls for an immediate shutdown of this facility and a thorough investigation of the premises. If you'll stand aside, ma'am, I would like to start that investigation right now."

I put my arm around Grandma. Her shoulders trembled.

I let Grandma go and stepped in front of her and faced Tate, my heart beating wildly.

"Do you have a search warrant?" I asked.

His smile disappeared. "You're in no position to ask me questions, boy."

"Do you have a search warrant?"

"Well, no. But as this petition clearly states—"

"You and I both know that petition wouldn't stand up in a court of law," I said. At least I hoped it wouldn't. I was just saying what I'd heard in police movies. This was no time to show weakness or uncertainty, though. "If you come back with a warrant, then we'll have to let you in. But if you don't have one, you can sit out on the lawn with everyone else." I hoped my voice didn't sound as shaky as it felt.

Tate bent down, stuck his face within a few inches of mine. "You see that crowd, boy? If they decide they want to come in here, they sure won't be using any warrants."

Tate made a horrible sound in his throat, then turned and spat a gob of phlegm on Grandma's porch before settling his eyes on me again. How could Amy possibly share even one atom of DNA with this guy?

"I'm the only one who can control that mob, so working with me's the only way to guarantee no one gets hurt. You hear me?" He glanced at his watch. "Now, it's almost noon. You got one hour to round up your Grandma and any of her customers and bring 'em out front, real peaceable-like. You have my word they won't be harmed. But I'll be taking them to the station and closing down this business, for good. That's the best deal you're gonna get. After that, well…whatever happens, happens. You understand?"

The sheriff stood back up to his full height and crossed his arms over his chest.

"You got one hour."

22

I checked my watch every thirty seconds or so. The minutes remaining till Tate's deadline ticked by in my head as I tried to think of something I could do as we waited for the Intergalactic Police Force to arrive.

Unfortunately, they were about the only people who *hadn't* shown up. Every resident of Forest Grove seemed to be out front, forming a massive mob that filled up the streets as well as the sidewalk. The crowd spilled over the fence and right into the front yard.

People were getting noisy, restless. Some waved signs that said things like FOREST GROVE IS FOR HUMANS AND TREES ONLY, and EXTREMELY ILLEGAL ALIENS NOT WELCOME HERE. Some of them threw things at the house when Tate wasn't looking.

And it wasn't just the locals we had to worry about. Big white vans with satellite dishes on top rose above the crowd like stones in the Nooksack River, the lettering on their sides a jumble of alphabet soup: KIRO, KOMO, KING, KCPQ. All the Seattle television stations. The people who climbed out carried big lights and cameras, which they either pointed at the house or used to interview the citizens.

The camera crews all had big umbrellas set up over their equipment. Huge, dark clouds had been blowing across the sky all morning. When that happened around here, the sun was completely blotted out, and the sky got an eerie, dusky look in the middle of the day.

Grandma, Mr. Harnox, and I huddled together in the sitting room, trying to brainstorm a way out of this mess. We took turns peeking out the windows. Right now it was Grandma's turn.

"Oh, great galaxies, there he goes," she muttered.

"What's he doing now?" I asked. We didn't even need to use Tate's name anymore.

"He's on that bullhorn again. Some nonsense about 'Is this the type of place we want in our community?' and 'Vigilance is the only way we can be sure that our children are safe.'" She did a pretty good imitation of his gruff, self-important voice. "I swear, that man is doing everything but handing out the torches and pitchforks. And it's funny, isn't it, how he only seems to fire up the speeches when one of those TV cameras gets near him."

I grunted and drummed my fingers on the chair's armrest. I was having serious trouble picturing a scenario where all of this ended well. What could the Intergalactic Police Force possibly do, anyway? Would they just make things worse? I was coming to the realization that maybe the arrival of *more* aliens wasn't the solution to this problem.

But what if they didn't show up? What then?

I had been racking my brain for a Plan B but was coming up blank every time. I checked my watch. Again. Fifty minutes left.

Grandma turned to look at me. "Scrub? Honey, are you okay?" I shrugged. "As okay as can be expected, I mean?"

"It's probably just my stomach." We hadn't eaten breakfast or lunch. Too nervous. "Speaking of torches and pitchforks, maybe we should get the house ready for a worst-case scenario. You know, board up the windows, maybe push some furniture up against the doors?"

Grandma just shook her head sadly. "If those people decide they want to come in, they'll find a way in. We won't keep them out by force."

I knew she was right.

Grandma looked out the window again. Mr. Harnox caught my eye, then stood up and silently motioned toward the hallway.

I followed and met him near the kitchen door. "What's up?" I whispered.

"Little man...you know I wish no pain to the humans... none of the suffering, yes?"

I craned my neck to look up at him and nodded.

He held up one long and twisty finger. "However...if they come inside...and try to do the harm to your ancestor-woman..." He fixed me with a stare. "I will stop them." My breath caught in my throat. "I stop them hard. Are you understanding this?"

I nodded again. I understood too well.

I remembered the effortless way he had plucked the two big teenagers off the ground and held them in the air. My imagination conjured up a horrible scene: the mob rushing the house, Mr. Harnox on the porch, scooping up grown men and hurling them back into the crowd, mowing down the citizens of Forest Grove like bowling pins. People could be killed, probably *would* be killed. Grandma losing her business would be the least of anybody's worries.

Oh, man. This was getting worse and worse. "Look, just sit with Grandma right now, okay? Don't do anything until I tell you. Okay?"

Mr. Harnox nodded and walked back to the sitting room. I paced up and down the length of the hallway, taking deep breaths. I glanced at my watch. Forty-six minutes until the deadline. Forty-six minutes until the riot starts. Oh, man. My stomach was so knotted up with worry that I felt like throwing up.

Suddenly an idea came to me. A desperate idea, and not a very good one. But I had to do something.

I ran upstairs to my room and rifled through my junk drawer. There—buried underneath a pile of alien coins—Tate's crumpled up business card, the one he had given me the day I met him at the grocery store.

I sat on the edge of the bed and studied the phone number. Maybe he'd listen to reason, I told myself. Maybe if he agreed to break up the mob, send everyone home, then we could let him in and at least talk to him, make some sort of compromise. I couldn't think of what that might look like, but the only thing that mattered at the moment was getting all of those angry people out of here, defusing the situation and avoiding any violence.

I clutched the card and tiptoed down the stairs. After peeking in and making sure that Grandma and Mr. Harnox were still in the sitting room, I snuck into one of the front rooms that had a phone.

I took a deep breath, rehearsed my opening lines a few times in my head, and dialed the number.

"Hello?" The voice was muted, hard to make out.

"Sheriff Tate, this is Scrub, the boy inside the bed-and-breakfast." I rushed the words, trying to get him to hear me before he said no. "Please listen to me. I don't want anyone to get hurt, so I'm asking you—"

"Scrub? Is that you?" Definitely not Tate's voice.

"Yeah…"

The voice was louder this time, but still hushed. "Scrub, it's me. Amy." Even with everything that was happening, it still felt good to hear her voice.

"Amy! Hey, why are you answering this call? Where are you?"

"I'm in my dad's patrol car." I carried the phone to the window and peeked out. Tate's patrol car sat at the edge of the crowd, where the street turned into a dead end.

"I don't see you."

"I'm lying down on the floor. I just... I can't stand to watch what's going on out there." Her voice broke. "But I couldn't just stay home, either." She was silent for a moment. "Why are you calling my dad?"

"I'm trying to keep things from getting ugly."

"Too late. Things are already ugly."

"I know, it's just... I'm afraid that if I don't do something, people are going to get hurt. Or worse. I think—"

"Scrub, I need to tell you something. I wasn't sure I was going to— Oh, never mind all that. Just listen to me very closely." Amy's voice had changed. It was more urgent, and she sounded more sure of herself. "I overheard my dad talking to his deputy. He's planning to storm the house with as many people from the mob who will follow him." I watched Tate circling through the crowd, handing out copies of *The Forest Grove Gazette* and pointing at the house with a scowl on his face.

"How do you—"

"Just listen. He knows he's being watched, especially with those TV cameras out here. He's going to climb up on the porch and give a big speech to get people riled up. That's the signal for his deputy to sneak around the back of your grandma's house and fire his gun in the air. When the shot goes off, my dad will have an excuse to take action. People will figure the shot's coming from inside the house, and then when he runs to the front door his supporters will follow him."

I looked from the window to where Grandma clutched at Mr. Harnox. "That sneaky jerk, I'll—"

"Don't talk like that about my dad."

"Why not? He's—"

"Scrub. He's my dad."

"Then why are you trying to help me?" This was getting very complicated.

"He's my dad and I believe him. I just don't believe *in* him right now."

"Huh?"

"He's doing this all the wrong way. He should be— Never mind. Look, I just needed to tell you so you could make sure everyone in there is safe. I keep trying to talk to him about leaving, doing this another way, but he won't listen to me."

"Well, can you at least try to stall him?"

"I'll do what I can, but—"

"Amy! He's headed for the car!"

Click. The line went dead. I watched from the window as Amy jumped out of the car, just as Sheriff Tate opened the door. She started talking, waving her hands in the air, while he stood and frowned at her, arms crossed on top of his big belly.

I set down the phone and walked back into the sitting room. Grandma was at the window, shaking her head and clucking her tongue. "All of those people out there. Who would have thought? I've spent my life running an inn for space aliens, and yet this is the most surreal thing I've ever seen. It's like a bad movie."

A lightbulb went on in my brain. I suddenly knew what to do. That's all it took, those two words. *Bad movie.*

I looked at my watch. Forty-one minutes left on Tate's deadline, if he honored it. I had to act fast.

"Grandma, stay here and watch things out front, okay? I think I can fix this."

"But what are you—"

"Just trust me, okay?"

I searched her eyes and saw the trust that I feared I would never see again. "You be careful. And let me know if you need my help."

"Thanks, Grandma." I ran down the hall and out the back door.

23.

I snuck out to the backyard. The forest closed in on Grandma's house, leaving only a narrow walkway on each side and shielding me from the view of all the gawkers out front.

I made it to the storage sheds and grabbed a double armload of supplies. Three trips up and down the stairs later, a pile of everything I needed sat in the middle of my room. Newspaper, cardboard, a string of Christmas lights, an oversize tub of Elmer's glue, a package of long, skinny balloons, a bag of flour, and some paint. Also the Complete Stage Makeup and

Accessories Kit for Tourist disguises. I sat on the floor and got to work, trying to ignore the crowd noise underneath the window.

I hadn't made a papier-mâché project since first grade and had forgotten how messy it can get. I had also forgotten how bad I am at making papier-mâché projects.

I checked my watch as I worked. The minutes rushed by much too quickly. The light coming in through the window was definitely getting duller with the threat of thundershowers. When there were ten minutes left, I had almost finished, but some parts were still goopy and damp. I rushed to the bathroom and brought back two hair dryers to speed up the drying process. It was a good thing I had used mostly glue; real papier-mâché takes forever to dry.

And then I was out of time. I appraised my work. The cardboard was cut sort of crooked; the papier-mâché looked lumpy in too many spots; and the paint colors didn't exactly match the original.

But it would have to do.

24

I crept down the stairs, cradling my project with both arms. Grandma and Mr. Harnox were in the sitting room, huddled together, peeking out the front windows. I shuffled down the hall, eased myself through the swinging door, then slipped through the kitchen and out the back door.

I shut the door as quietly as I could and stepped onto the back porch. All of those black clouds made the daytime feel like twilight, and a steady gust of wind pushed against me.

I set everything down in a pile on the porch, then

picked up one piece at a time and started putting it on. When everything was in place, I used a window as a mirror. I turned in circles, looking at myself from all angles. The Jungle Boys would die from their chittering laughter if they saw me like this, but it was now or never.

The timing had to be just right. I wanted to be in position when Tate started to—

"May I have your attention, please?" The sheriff's voice boomed through the bullhorn from the other side of the house. "Some of you may not believe in creatures from the depths of space." The bullhorn amplified his drawl so that it filled up the darkening sky. "But I have served this community faithfully, and I tell you today that I have seen what I have seen!" I could hear the crowd respond to that out front, a swell of murmured approval. "And I have photographic evidence to back it up!" He received applause and a few cheers.

I started down the back porch steps, then stopped. I scanned the backyard, looking for Tisdall, Tate's little deputy. I couldn't afford to run into him before I could get out front and carry out my plan. Tate droned on as I squinted into the backyard, which was covered in shadows.

"We've all seen the peculiar goings-on at this place of business over the years, have we not?" Some shouts of approval from the mob. "The weird-looking guests that stroll though our town, talking strange and acting more than a little bit off. Am I right?" More shouts and whistles from the other side of the house.

No sign of Tisdall. The plan could have changed—maybe Tate thought he could get the crowd ready to charge by himself, without the warning shot from his deputy. I reached the bottom of the steps and braced myself for action.

"Now, I don't pretend to know everything that's going on here, folks," Tate said. "But I do know this: even though this bed-and-breakfast is always full of strange customers... there never seems to be a single car parked out front. You ever notice that, my friends? Have you ever seen a car here? Now just how can that be?"

More whistles and catcalls. I had a moment of panic when I didn't think I was going to be able to go through with it after all.

But then an image of Grandma came to me, huddled inside and watching through the window, terrified of what might happen. I *had* to make this up to her. That helped me focus.

"So I guess the question I have to ask all of you is this," Tate bellowed. "Whether or not you believe in life on other planets..." He paused. I took a deep breath and readied myself.

"...is this really the kind of establishment we want in our town?"

A roar of "No!" Tate had done his job. Signal or no signal, that crowd sounded ready to move. Time for me to act.

I reached behind me and switched on the battery pack. The Christmas lights blinked on. Now or nev—

"What the...?"

The voice startled me so badly, my heart stopped. I turned to look, and there was Tisdall, across the backyard. He stepped out from the shadow of a storage shed and into the gloomy pre-storm light.

He gaped at me, his mouth hanging open and his eyes wide.

We stared at each other for a moment.

And then I noticed that his gun wasn't pointed at the sky, ready to take a warning shot. He gripped that gun in two shaking hands, and it was pointed right at me.

I realized that maybe this wasn't the best plan in the world.

My legs were frozen in place. Even when Tisdall started running straight at me, yelling something incoherent, I couldn't move. I couldn't yell. I couldn't breathe.

He closed the gap quickly, each step bringing him closer and closer. I was so scared that I couldn't even close my eyes or cover my face with my hands. I was doomed to just stand there and watch the end of it all. The end of me.

I was dimly aware of the sound of the crowd members out front, yelling and chanting themselves into a deafening, senseless fury. I had time to say a silent prayer that Grandma would somehow be okay even though my plan had backfired and I had failed her and she might never see me alive again—when Tisdall tripped over a croquet mallet and fell face-first in the grass. When his body hit the ground, his arm flailed around, and the gun went off with a roar that sounded like a cannon.

My ears were ringing from the explosion, but I could still hear a few things from out front. Someone screamed, and then Tate yelled into his bullhorn. "We're under attack! Follow me!"

My legs started to work again.

25

I raced around the side of the house, my legs churning underneath all of the cardboard and papier-mâché. The mob surged toward the house, Tate in the lead. I dashed around the front porch, waving my hands over my head. I hadn't rehearsed any good noises, so I just let fly with a "Whoo-oo-oo!" like a Halloween ghost.

The first person to see me was a big woman in a pink housedress. Sometimes when little kids fall down, they're so surprised they open up their mouths to cry and no sound comes out for a few seconds.

That's exactly how she looked: her eyes the size of headlights, her mouth open in the scream face with no sound coming out. But then, just like that hurt little kid, her lungs caught up to her, and she belted out the loudest shriek I've ever heard. Everyone in the crowd turned at the same instant, and there were more screams, and then everything happened at once.

The crowd scene became total chaos. Some people ran left, some right, others in circles. Eddie and Brian bumped into each other and pinballed off to run suddenly in opposite directions. The picket fence was flattened as the mob surged away from the house. A crowd of people split off and ran down the street toward town, with Deputy Tisdall out in front, waving his hands in the air and screaming.

Parents grabbed small children in protective hugs. More than a few people crawled underneath their lawn chairs and put their hands over their heads as if in an elementary school hurricane drill. Screams filled the air.

Tate yelled into his bullhorn. "Stand back, citizens! Stand back!" He ran straight toward me, the bullhorn bouncing in front of his face. "I won't let this one bring danger to Forest Grove!"

The crowd fanned out, everyone scrambling to get into the street. They encircled the yard, leaving only me and the sheriff in the middle.

Tate tossed his bullhorn on the grass and ran with both arms outstretched to grab me. I led him around the perimeter of the lawn, dodging behind obstacles—a bush or a spaceship sculpture—only to race back out a different way.

But the mob formed an impenetrable wall around us, and there was only so much zigging and zagging I could do.

When I turned to head back to the middle of the lawn, the sheriff crashed into me from behind.

I stumbled and landed facedown on the grass. Tate landed on top of me, and it felt like I'd never be able to breathe again.

"Gotcha!" Tate yelled. He pushed his way off of me and stood up. "Citizens of Forest Grove, I give you proof of the alien presence that menaces our town!"

Tate grabbed my shoulders and tried to yank me upright, but when he did, my headpiece and mask popped off.

The crowd gasped. Tate was left holding a replica of a papier-mâché Jungle Boy head high in the air. He gaped at the mask. It was painted brown and green and had a mass of thinly cut cardboard strips bobbing on top like those growths on the alien boys' heads. Then he looked down at me. His eyes grew round and huge.

The crowd was silent for several moments. Then someone yelled, "Look, an arm fell off that thing."

People moved closer, squinting at us. "Wait a minute, I think those are Christmas lights. You can see the cable right there."

"Those claws on the feet look like plastic forks. I think they're painted green."

"The whole thing's held together with duct tape and Band-Aids."

Tate looked from me to the crowd, an outraged expression on his face. He started shaking his head slowly.

Everyone shouted at once.

"That's not an alien!"

"It's just someone in a costume."

"It's only a kid!"

"Wait—I think I recognize him under the face paint. It's that new kid, the one who works here. I've seen him around town."

Tate raised his hands for silence. He tossed the Jungle Boy headpiece aside and glared down at me.

"Just what do you think you're doing, boy?"

Everyone got real quiet then. I looked out at the assembled crowd.

I was taken back for a moment to second grade and that disastrous Robin Hood play. I could actually feel the relentless glare of the audience burning into me. It had been the worst moment of my life, everyone laughing and staring and pointing, right at *me*.

I stared at all of those faces in the crowd and froze up. I didn't know if I could finish the job.

But then I looked over at the window, at Grandma peering out at the front lawn. The person who trusted me to be able to end this.

I turned back to the mob, cleared my throat, and tried to speak loudly enough for everyone to hear.

"I thought it would be good for my grandma's business," I said. "I mean, when I hiked out to your campsite last night to spook you and the Scouts, it was just a prank. But when I got my picture in the newspaper, and everyone started making such a big deal about it, I figured it would be good advertising. Any publicity is good publicity, right?"

The crowd groaned. Tate stared at me with his mouth wide open.

"What a waste of time," said an elderly woman with three cameras strapped around her neck.

"I knew it was a hoax all along," said a man in denim overalls. There were grass stains on his knees from when he had cowered under a lawn chair.

Splat! I got pegged with a half-eaten apple, right in the chest, and little chunks splattered my face. Then a banana peel, a rotten pear, a half-empty Coke can, and two hot dogs still in their sloppy buns.

The humiliation was a million times worse than being in that stupid play. This was real life.

Tate's face went as red as the ketchup smeared on my costume. He turned to address the crowd. "But—but—but this is not what I saw last night!" he yelled. This announcement was met with a hearty chorus of booing. "I promise you, all of you, it was a real alien last night!"

The people near us shook their heads, turned away, and walked off. "I knew we shouldn't have believed him," said a bearded man with a cane. "This is ridiculous."

"I can understand the Cub Scouts getting fooled; they're just kids," his female companion grumbled. "But you're a grown man, Sheriff." She too walked away from the scene and down the street.

"Wait! Listen to me! Please!" Tate pleaded. "There were more of them! And—and—and they were real! They didn't look anything like this! They were real, I tell you!" Tate spun in circles, trying to find anyone who would believe him, but the crowd grew thinner and thinner. Parents pulled their children away in wagons, others pushed bikes down the street, and the TV crews packed up their vans and rumbled off.

Well over half of the crowd had left. Tate grabbed at a couple of the armed men who had trailed him all day. "Come on, you guys. Let's search this place." They looked at each other uncertainly. "Listen, this place was full of guests this morning. They couldn't've just disappeared. Come on!"

Tate lumbered up the steps, followed by three of the men. Some of the remaining members of the crowd stayed and watched them; others trickled away, still shaking their heads.

Grandma opened the door wide. She was smiling. "Be my guest, Sheriff."

I followed. Tate staggered through the house, opening doors that led to empty rooms and transporters that looked like closets.

When he had blown through the entire house, he mounted the steps for another tour. But the three guys with him shooed him off and headed for the front door. One of them even touched his cap and nodded once at Grandma on his way out. "Sorry to disturb you, ma'am."

Tate followed them onto the porch, where a small crowd still watched from the lawn. "But—but what about *him*?" The sheriff pointed at Mr. Harnox, sitting calmly in his suit on one of Grandma's deck chairs. He waved to the people on the lawn.

"Leave him alone, Tate," someone called.

"You've wasted enough time and taxpayer money for one night," someone else said. "You should be down at the school trying to catch the kids that've been spray-painting their crazy pictures on the brick walls down there."

The men who had followed Tate into the bed-and-breakfast collected their wives and kids and took off down the street toward town.

In a matter of minutes, the crowd was gone. Even though

my face still burned from the embarrassment I had suffered, the rest of me swelled with triumph. My plan had actually worked! And there was nothing the sheriff could do about it now.

Tate stood alone on the grass, surrounded by a sea of food wrappers and discarded newspapers. I thought he would be furious, that he might even try to climb the steps to the porch to attack me. But after one glance at him, I knew I didn't have to worry about that.

The first heavy drops of rain fell then, spattering Tate's hat and uniform. His shoulders drooped and his head hung loosely on his neck as he stared at the ground. It looked like he had shrunk half a foot. He didn't move. If he'd had a shred of decency I might have even felt a little bit sorry for him.

I turned to the front door. Grandma held it open for me. "They're all gone," I said.

"I know. That was very brave, David."

"David?"

She put her hand on my shoulder. "Do you mind if I call you that? 'Scrub' is endearing, but anyone brave and resourceful enough to do all of that deserves a better name."

I thought for a moment, then nodded. "Sounds good to me."

She stepped aside to let me enter. I turned to take a last look at Tate.

Amy now stood in the middle of the yard, staring up at me. I couldn't read her facial expression through the gloom and rain. She took her father by the hand and silently led him to his car.

26

ALIEN SIGHTING REVEALED AS HOAX

SHERIFF, PRANKSTER TO FACE DISCIPLINARY ACTION

FOREST GROVE—An alleged alien sighting reported by Whatcom County Sheriff Robert Tate was debunked when the prankster attempted to strike a second time last week.

The practical joker, costumed minor David "Scrub" Elliott of Tampa, Florida, crashed a rally led by Tate in the late evening. Hundreds of local citizens had gathered to hear Tate's theories on the "alien" that he believed was connected with a colorful local inn, the Intergalactic Bed and Breakfast.

Many members of the assembled crowd later claimed they had attended the rally as a joke, but the County Council sees this as no laughing matter.

"The sheriff's actions were irresponsible, inexcusable, and, quite frankly, embarrassing," said County Council president, Dale Mount. Tate has been suspended indefinitely pending an investigation into the matter and runs the risk of losing his job permanently.

Elliott, in town for the summer to work at the inn, will have to answer for his actions as well. He has been cited for disorderly conduct and faces up to 100 hours of community service and (story continued on page B4)

27

My little stunt with the alien costume was captured by plenty of video cameras, and the footage has been watched over three million times and counting on YouTube. Also, I was the top News of the Weird segment on CNN, MSNBC, Fox News, and pretty much every regional TV newscast in America.

Even though I spent my fifteen minutes of fame as a nationwide laughingstock, it was still kind of cool. I walked down to the library one day to use the Internet, and when I typed my name into the major search engines I got hundreds of posts.

But any hope I might've had for leaving my public humiliation behind in Forest Grove when I traveled home disappeared when Tyler Sandusky sent me a postcard. I think it's
the first time that guy has ever actually snail-mailed anything
in his life. On the front was a typical touristy picture of a
family playing on the beach in Florida. But Tyler had taken
a green Sharpie and drawn Vulcan ears on the kids, antennae
popping out of the parents' heads, things like that. On the
back, the message read: *I sent the link to your video to everyone in
my e-mail address book. The Sci-Fi/Fantasy Club just held elections
for president-and-supreme-ruler-for-life and you won in a landslide.
Congratulations!*

At least there was a chance that Tyler was kidding. The
e-mail from my mom—which accused me of bringing public disgrace to the family name and threatened punishments
of epic proportions upon my return home—sounded a little
more serious.

But I didn't really let either one of them get to me. Sure,
it was going to take some time to live down this embarrassment (and to convince my mom to ever let me leave the house
again), but it had all been worth it to see that look on Tate's
face when he knew he'd been beaten.

There wasn't time to dwell on my personal problems anyway. I spent four hours a day cleaning up litter around Forest
Grove to fulfill my community-service duties. It was lonely
work; people actually crossed to the other side of the street
to avoid me. They shook their heads and muttered from the
opposite sidewalk as they walked past.

But even though I was a social outcast in town, I was a hero
inside the Intergalactic Bed and Breakfast. Grandma was

always making a big fuss over me and telling me how proud she was. Now that it was just the three of us, she cooked my favorite foods—or at least the organic, non-processed equivalent. We spent a lot of time cleaning and repairing the inn, but we also had time to just hang out. Me, Grandma, and Mr. Harnox played cards or board games every night. It was actually more fun than it sounds, kind of a real summer vacation after all.

The Intergalactic Police Force never did show up, but the transporters had been shut down remotely, just as Grandma had feared. This meant there was no way to contact them to let them know the crisis was over. I was starting to get worried that Grandma would never be able to start up her business again.

Her *real* business, that is. One of the unexpected side effects from all of the press coverage was that her phone had been ringing off the hook with people calling from every state and even other countries. Everyone wanted to stay the night at the quirky space place made famous on TV.

But Grandma didn't accept a single offer for a human customer; she even had the phone changed to an unlisted number. She seemed perfectly happy and said she was glad to finally have some downtime to fix up the place. Whenever I asked her whether she was worried about ever being able to reopen her business, she would just smile and say, "The universe will provide. It always has, and I imagine it always will."

One day, we were sitting on the floor of a bare guest room, stirring up a gluey mixture to spread on the back of wallpaper before we put it up. Grandma was humming happily to herself.

"So . . . Grandma?"

"Hmmmm?"

"Have you given any more thought to letting in some of the people—you know, the humans—who want to stay here now?"

"Not really, no." She didn't look up from where she was laying out the wallpaper in flat sheets.

"Because you could probably fill every room here, every night, for the next decade or so. You know, with all of the people that have been calling."

"I suppose."

I kept pressing. "And you could probably charge a lot more, with the demand so high."

"Mmmm-mmmm."

"In fact, you could probably make enough money in about six months to retire. Do you ever think about that, about retiring? I mean, you've done this for over forty years. And I've seen how much energy it takes to run this place. Maybe having the transporters shut down could finally give you an excuse to start relaxing."

Grandma gave me a strange look and stood up. "Follow me," she said.

We walked downstairs, out the back door and onto the lawn, where Grandma opened up a pair of rough exterior doors. I followed her out of the sunshine and down a staircase into the cool, dim cellar below.

"What are we doing down here?" I said.

"Here—help me move these boxes out of the way."

We scooted a tower of cardboard boxes around until there was an aisle to walk through. Grandma led me to where two trunks sat against the back wall. "Open them," she said.

I popped the latch on the first one and lifted the lid. It was crammed full with yellowish chunks of rock. There must have been, I don't know, maybe a hundred pounds of it. My mouth fell open. "Gold?" I asked when my brain started working again.

Grandma nodded. "Now the other one."

I lifted the lid. This one held diamonds. They were rough and uncut, but still diamonds. And they were huge. One chunk on top was almost as big as a basketball. I wasn't sure exactly how many dollars something like that would be worth, but it had to be a number with a whole lot of commas between a whole lot of zeroes.

"But this . . . this is . . . how did you . . . ?"

Grandma laughed. "Come on. Let's talk out in the sunshine." After I was able to pry my eyes away from all that loot, I closed the trunks. We shuffled the boxes back into place and then walked up the stairs to the backyard. Grandma sat on a rocking chair on the back porch, and I flopped down on one of the steps.

Grandma raised one eyebrow at me. "A pretty good retirement plan, don't you think, David?"

"Yeah, I think that should cover it," I said. "How did you get all of that?"

"An interplanetary trader transports in every year or so. He swaps goods all over the cosmos. He might swing by a planet where gold or diamonds are so common that they have no monetary value whatsoever. They're just rocks. So he'll scoop them up and bring a load here to trade."

"What do you give him?"

Grandma smiled. "You know that alien money you've

been getting as tips all summer? I have barrels full of it. The trader can exchange it on other planets. So I hand over a chest full of alien currency and get a pile of diamonds or gold in return. We both shake hands and part happily."

"Wow. What a great racket. You're rich!"

"I suppose. But having a lot of Earth money doesn't really help in my business." She sighed. "All the gold in that cellar can't entice a single transporter repairman to spend a few weeks on a primitive planet to help me out."

"But it can help you when you want to retire," I said.

Grandma didn't answer.

"I guess you don't really feel like retiring yet, huh?"

"I don't think so, David." She rocked back and forth in her chair. "It's always been such a delight, having the Tourists here. And this has been much more than a job for me all of these years. You could say it's been my life's purpose."

"Oh yeah?"

"If I can offer a place where species of all kinds can mingle in peace, then that's the greatest gift I can offer the cosmos. It fills me with such hope for all of us."

I thought back to the day the angry mob almost rushed the inn, and I sighed. "Too bad other people don't see it the same way."

She looked at me with sad eyes. "You miss the girl, don't you? Amy?"

I swallowed, and nodded. "Every time I try to call, Tate answers. He hangs up when I ask to talk to her. The phone book has an address for their house, but I don't dare go over there."

Grandma nodded. "There's another reason I've stayed

open all of this time, but it's silly, I suppose. And gets sillier every year." She picked up a forgotten teacup from the floor and stared into it for a while before continuing. "When I first opened the inn I had just graduated from the Evergreen State College. I was so young, just a foolish girl. Then I met a Tourist who helped me—"

"How *did* you meet your first Tourist?" I asked. I had been so busy dealing with present-day aliens all this time that it had never occurred to me to ask how it all started.

"That's a very long story, and one for another time," Grandma said. "But this Tourist opened my eyes to the worlds beyond Earth, and he helped me set this place up. It was his idea, actually, to hide out in the open with all of the space-themed accoutrements. He had a marvelous sense of humor." Grandma was quiet for a moment, and this time the smile briefly touched her eyes.

"We became quite close, very dear friends. He was forced to leave about a year after we opened this place. The truth is, part of me hopes that someday he'll come walking out of one of those transporters. Yes, I admit it, that's part of the reason I've kept at this so long."

Grandma got a faraway look in her eyes after that. Whatever she was thinking about was somehow making her face look younger.

And then I clued in to what she might have been thinking about, and I shuddered all over. I had to get up and walk around the backyard to get the willies out.

There was only one thing worse than thinking about your own grandmother . . . *in that way* . . . with any guy in the world. And that was thinking about your grandmother with an alien.

We continued to work on the house, and I pulled double shifts on Forest Grove cleanup duty to finish up my community-service hours. The back-to-school sales hit the newspaper ads and TV commercials, a sign that my time at Grandma's place was nearing an end.

One Sunday evening, Grandma, Mr. Harnox, and I sat in the living room, playing dominoes. It was hard for me to concentrate.

"Are you feeling okay, David? It's your turn," Grandma said.

I shifted my gaze from the game and looked up at her. "I've been thinking about your story, Grandma. About waiting and waiting for your friend to come through that transporter?" She nodded. I stood up. "I'm sorry to run, but there's something I just have to do. Even if it doesn't work."

Grandma smiled and reached over to pat my hand. "Do what you feel is right."

I crossed to the front door; I didn't care what Tate would do to me. I had to see Amy, even if it was just for one more time. I went out the door and was about to run down the steps when I heard the front gate bang. And there was Amy, breathless and clutching some kind of binder.

I hurried down the steps to meet her. "Hey. I was just on my way to see you and—"

She held up her hand for me to stop. "I only have a minute or two." She forced the words out while trying to catch her breath. She scanned the block, then turned to me. Everything I wanted to say to her over the last few weeks got jumbled up in my head, and I didn't know where to begin. "I came to tell you we're leaving town," she said.

"Leaving? Why? You've lived here your whole life."

"My dad lost his job."

We were quiet after that. She stared at her sandals. Part of me just couldn't believe that I would never see her again.

I forced myself to say something. I couldn't just stand here until she turned around to leave for good. "Where are you going?"

"We're moving to Bothell, outside of Seattle. Dad got a job at this mall as a night security guard. It was the only... the only job that..." Tears brimmed in Amy's eyes. Without thinking I wrapped my arms around her and pulled her close. The floodgates opened. She shook and sobbed.

"Oh, you should see him... hasn't left the house... sits around in his bathrobe... still listens to the police scanner all night... being sheriff only thing... ever wanted... even worse... than when Mom left."

She buried her wet face in my T-shirt and I held her. I whispered that it was going to be okay, even though I didn't believe it.

Her sobs softened after a while, and she was able to catch a few shaky breaths. She stepped back, wiped at her eyes, and brushed her hair out of her face. "I ran down here while he was packing up the truck. He could be here any second." We looked at each other. Fresh tears shone on her cheeks in the moonlight. "I just wanted to say good-bye. I'm really going to miss you."

"I'll miss you too," I said, trying to control my shaky voice.

"But I also wanted you to have this." She put the binder in my hands. "I know you did what you had to do. And I don't blame you. But I wanted you to have this...so you'd know." It was a photo album, an old thing with duct tape holding the spine together. The opening pages had three photos glued in: the sign in front of the bed-and-breakfast; rocking chairs on the front porch; windows on the top floor. The edges of each picture showed blurry leaves, evidence that the photographer had been hiding in some bushes.

Not understanding, I looked at Amy. She nodded. "Go on."

I flipped to the next page, a shot of Grandma on the back porch talking to two of her guests. One of them had pointy ears and a rainbow-colored face. The other was only two feet tall, but he was eye-to-eye with Grandma, since he was floating three feet in the air. The next picture showed two creatures, their bodies covered in wisps of long green hair. They were eating a rocking chair. The next picture was a guest climbing a tree. His four muscular arms were tailor-made for climbing, and he was trying not to bump the branches with the stegosauruslike spikes running down his back. I flipped through the rest of the photo album—all shots of Tourists.

"You knew?" It came out in a whisper.

She nodded.

"But—but—but—you *knew*? Everything? Coming over for breakfast...and Mr. Harnox...and the night in the woods. You knew it all? The whole time?"

She nodded again. "I figured it out a couple of years ago. I used to come over here every day after school and just hide in the bushes and watch."

"Why?"

"I didn't know anything about what was really going on for a long time. But the place was so fascinating anyway. Your grandma's the most interesting person in this little town. And she's so brave. She just does whatever she wants and doesn't care what anybody thinks of her. I admire her so much—it's the main reason that I told you about my dad's plan to rush the bed-and-breakfast that night. I couldn't let that happen to her."

My mind was almost as numb as when I learned about the aliens for the first time. But Amy looked back down the street, and I knew time was running out. I forced myself to focus. "Why didn't you tell your dad?"

"Oh, I knew how he'd react. He wasn't ready. I've been hoping he'd be ready someday...but after that whole mob scene..." Amy swiped at a tear.

Suddenly a dark pickup truck sped down the street, with a jumble of suitcases and furniture bungee-corded in the back. Tires screeched as the truck came to a sudden stop in front of the house. Amy whispered fiercely into my ear, "Don't worry, Scrub. Your grandma's secret is safe with me. I'll never tell him. I'll never tell anyone." The truck door opened. Heavy footsteps fell on the sidewalk. "Living close to your grandma's place has been the best thing that ever happened to me. It's helped me to see that anything is possible," Amy said quickly. She wiped back some more tears and hugged me again. "I don't want to go."

I hardly recognized the man who walked through the gate. He wore an old baseball cap. His face was covered with a week's growth of whiskers. Clearly, he had not slept much. He stared at me.

I expected yelling. Swear words. Threats. But all Tate said was, "Time to go."

Amy nodded to her father. She looked back at me and tapped the photo album. "Keep it."

I wanted to say thanks, but I didn't think I'd be able to force the words around the lump in my throat, so I hugged her.

"Will you take your hands off my daughter?" Tate stepped forward, reaching for me.

The front door flew open. "Don't you lay a hand on my grandson!" Grandma said, hurrying down the steps. Grandma and the sheriff glared at each other for a long moment, before Tate dropped his gaze and looked at his daughter.

"Come on, Amy," Tate said.

I couldn't believe this was really happening. Amy let go of me.

"Good-bye," she said.

"Bye." I choked on the word.

Watching Amy walk away, I felt a shiver, like the hair on the back of my neck was standing up. Suddenly great clouds of fog started rolling in. Even though there was no wind, the fog dropped down quickly, sinking below the tops of the trees until it nearly touched the ground. The road into town disappeared, and soon all I could see was the bottom floor of Grandma's place; the upper windows were just faint, blurry lights.

And what was that humming noise? It started so low I had to strain to hear it, but it got stronger, its intensity pulsing rhythmically. I couldn't decide if I was hearing it with my ears or feeling it with my body, or both. After a minute it was definitely throbbing in my chest, like standing next to a huge speaker with the bass pounding.

The hairs on my arms stood straight up. Amy's ponytail slowly rose until it was floating in the air. Tate tugged at his mustache in confusion. The ground trembled, sending tremors up through my legs that threw me off balance. I realized the entire house was shaking behind us, the shutters rattling in the window frames. A bright yellow light flashed in the sky, muted by the fog but still visible, blinking and fading in time with the throbbing, humming noise. The light turned purple, then red, then green, then some colors I didn't recognize, a kaleidoscope of colors.

Tate put his arm around Amy, backing toward the gate and clutching at his belt for the gun he no longer possessed. The fog-distorted colors played eerily across his face.

The pulsing hum sped up—I could feel it in my teeth now —and the ground shaking increased. My heart was pounding.

Then, all at once it stopped. The colors, the humming, everything. Amy's ponytail settled. I exhaled. Tate glared at me.

Mr. Harnox walked out onto the porch and looked up at the sky. We all followed his gaze. An enormous object was lowering toward us through the thick clouds. It dropped down, down, landing behind the house.

"Finally," Mr. Harnox said. A huge smile stretched across his face.

20

All of us raced to the backyard. The field behind
the house was totally obscured by a massive spaceship. The body of the ship looked like an enormous
metallic blimp supported by two oversize pontoons.
The part we could see, anyway. The top of the ship
was totally lost in the soupy fog, so who knows how
big it really was.

Still, it was too big for my field of vision. Thousands of round portals lined the blimp in horizontal
columns. The ship was jet black and sleek.

A massive tube stuck out the side, blowing fog

into the air. The shroud of clouds it had created all around Grandma's place would conceal it from anyone in town.

A last few traces of kaleidoscope colors zipped around the pontoons, fading in intensity until they finally switched off. The tip of one of the pontoons had landed on a storage shed, crumpling its roof, and some of the outbuildings were smashed completely.

"I knew it!" Tate said, his voice finding some of that self-assured gruffness again. "I've got you this time. You're not going to be able to dress up like *that* thing, boy." He grabbed a walkie-talkie from inside his jacket and started to make a call.

"Oh no, you don't," Grandma said, marching over to him and grabbing the device.

Tate clutched the walkie-talkie in a white-knuckled grip as he loomed above Grandma. She held on with both hands, locked in a tug-of-war. They might have pulled forever, but just then a tube dropped down from the underside of the craft and deposited two figures on the lawn. My heart hammered. These aliens were definitely not here for a vacation.

Tate positioned himself between the two aliens and Amy, grabbing her shoulders and moving her behind his broad back. Amy immediately poked her head out from behind his elbow in order to get a clear view.

One of the aliens stepped up to us. In the back porch lights we could see that he was short and slim with bright red skin. He wore a black uniform with geometric patterns outlined in white across the chest. He bent his body in what might have been a bow, then, with a sweeping gesture of his arm, indicated the alien coming up behind him. This one's head looked like a rectangular chunk of lime-green granite dropped directly on top of his massive, square shoulders. His block of a belly strained the fabric of his black uniform.

The little red alien spoke. "Presenting Commander Rezzlurr of the Intergalactic Police Force."

The huge green alien crossed his arms over his chest and stared at us. I swallowed dryly. Tate puffed himself up a little, straightened out his posture, almost like he was standing at attention. Maybe the ex-lawman in him recognized the presence of a superior officer.

"Received a distress call from your planet," the big alien rumbled. His little red underling fished a small device out of his pocket and pushed a button. A hologram of a spinning, blue-green globe appeared in the air, next to a column of scrolling words. Commander Rezzlurr glanced over at the hologram. "From your 'Earth.' Apparently you have an emergency."

It was Grandma, of course, who found her voice first. "We *had* an emergency, but it's over." She stepped forward to confront them, while the rest of us watched.

"We apologize for any inconvenience, ma'am," said the red alien.

Commander Rezzlurr shrugged. "It's a big galaxy."

"Well, now that you're finally here, at least you can turn my transporters back on. I have been unavailable for interstellar business the entire time we've been waiting."

The huge green alien shook his head, which must have been difficult with no neck. "Before we can do that we need to speak with your head of security," he said.

"Official protocol, ma'am," said the red alien.

"Head of security? But I don't have a head of security. I don't have any security."

Commander Rezzlurr nodded to the red alien, who punched numbers on his hologram device. The globe was replaced by a holographic image of Grandma's place. Rezzlurr looked at unrecognizable words scrolling by. "Says here you've been in business over forty years. You've gone all this time without hiring a head of security? I'll have to file that in my report."

"What are you talking about?"

The red alien hit another button and quoted from the fresh column of scrolling words. "'According to the law set down by the Interplanetary Collective, all transporter reception facilities are required to have at least one head of security who is either working or locally on-call twenty-four hours a day. Failure to comply may result in suspension or permanent loss of the facility's Interstellar Hotelier License.'"

"You can stop with the threats, if you don't mind. No one ever bothered to tell me about that rule," Grandma said.

"Terribly sorry, ma'am. Protocol." The red alien removed a stylus from his pocket and used it to write on his hologram machine; an image of a form filled the air in front of him, the words appearing as he scribbled on his machine. Commander Rezzlurr stood with his arms crossed, looking completely uninterested in the proceedings. "I'll need to get some information for the report," the red alien said.

"When can you open up the transporters again?" Grandma said.

"When we return to headquarters I will file the report. After that, a committee of authorities will review the facts and make their recommendation on reinstatement of the transporter system. If they decide on reinstatement, a representative will visit you the next time a service ship is in the area. There is a period of time where you may appeal any decision that—"

"*If* they decide on reinstatement? It'll be years before all of that happens!"

"If you had hired a proper head of security, perhaps the emergency could have been avoided," he said crisply. "Now, I need some information." He started with us males. "Name?" He looked at the tall gray alien.

"Harnox."

"Home planet and galaxy?"

"Shuunuu. Andromeda."

"Thank you." The stylus bobbed up and down in the red alien's fingers and the words scrawled out along the holographic form. He looked at me next. "Name?"

"Scrub—I mean David, David Elliott. Earth. Milky Way."

"Thank you. Name?"

Amy's father's hand moved to his head, and I think he was starting to salute, but then he dropped it. "Tate. Robert Tate."

The huge green alien got a strange look in his eye, staring into the distance and scratching his head. It looked like he was trying to remember something.

"You have to tell them your planet and galaxy, Dad," Amy said.

He paused a moment. "Right. This is Earth, and it's in the—"

· "Wait a minute," Commander Rezzlurr rumbled. "Did you say Tate? Robert Tate?"

Tate nodded, eyebrows crinkled in confusion.

Rezzlurr snatched the hologram device away from the red alien and jabbed at the console. The spinning globe reappeared, along with more writing. The green alien scanned through the words. "Did you post an official sighting with the National UFO Reporting Center in … let's see, here … Earth year 1977?"

Tate looked at the rest of us sheepishly, then studied his shoes.

"And did you describe the ship as … Where is it? … Oh, yes, here it is. 'A triangular body of wings encasing a large orb, flying in a zigzag pattern across the north sky?' Was that you?"

Tate coughed and quickly glanced at us again. "Sounds vaguely familiar."

A huge smile spread across Commander Rezzlurr's face. "That was an Arslaggian Slave Ship!" he cried. "I spent over a year chasing it all over the cosmos. Finally got so desperate I started checking the UFO reports from primitive planets. Sure enough, I stumbled across your posting. Those Arslaggian slimeballs were hiding out around here, thought no one would look for them in such a tiny solar system." Rezzlurr whacked Tate heartily on the back. "I finally caught up with them after your tip. Got my first promotion right afterward. Excellent police work."

Tate smiled proudly. Amy beamed. "Thank you … sir," Tate said.

"Oh no, it's me who needs to be thanking you. Wow. Running into Robert Tate, I just can't believe it. What a small universe, huh? So what do you do here, Tate?"

The smile disappeared. "Well, I spent many years as sheriff, but I recently...retired."

"Law enforcement? Excellent. And you say that you are currently in a state of self-deactivation? Even better."

Tate cleared his throat. "Well, my daughter and I will be moving soon to—"

"I'll cut right to the point, Tate," Rezzlurr said. "Would you consider reactivating? For a good cause?"

Tate looked at Amy, who beamed at him, then back at Rezzlurr. "I'm listening."

The huge green alien turned to Grandma. "I think we might have found your new head of security."

Grandma shook her head. "Oh no. I don't think so."

Rezzlurr ignored her. "What do you think, Tate? Would you like to become an official member of the Intergalactic Police Force?"

Tate's demeanor was all business. "What kind of salary and benefits are we looking at here, sir?"

The red alien chimed in. "You will have access to the finest health care in the universe. If you ever require medical attention, you simply transport to one of the health centers on—"

"That's right," rumbled Commander Rezzlurr. "You won't have to be subjected to the primitive techniques of the butchers on this backward planet, not anymore. Top of the line, Officer Tate. You'll probably double whatever the life expectancy is around here."

Grandma rolled her eyes at that one.

"And you get two weeks of paid vacation per quarter," the red alien continued. "If you wish, once per year you will be awarded an all-expenses-paid vacation to your choice of any of the tropical planets in the Adzerahrton Galaxy. They offer the finest—"

"The ladies there are something else," Rezzlurr interrupted, elbowing Tate in the ribs. "Thousands of species from all over, for every taste and—"

Tate cleared his throat more loudly and glanced at Amy beside him. "I think I get the point," he said.

Then he looked at the ground. We all watched him, waiting. Amy slipped her hand into his. "So . . . it would be a real law enforcement job?" he said.

"Sir," the little red alien said seriously, "you would have the most important law enforcement job on the planet."

Tate looked again at Amy, who squeezed his hand. Then he looked up at the aliens. "Ready, willing, and able."

"He'll be perfect," the big green alien said to Grandma. "The Collective likes security personnel to be native. Especially on primitive outposts."

Grandma shook her head again. "I'm sorry. We simply don't need any security around here."

Commander Rezzlurr frowned. "Oh really? I thought *you* called *us* about an important emergency."

The little red alien stepped in. "Ma'am? Hiring an approved security expert would mean that we could open up your transporters immediately." Commander Rezzlurr and Tate both smiled. The similarity in their expressions was a little unsettling. All of us, human and alien alike, stared at Grandma and awaited her answer. She crossed her arms and huffed.

Mr. Harnox bent down to her. "Excuse, but...you have told me oftentimes...that all of the creatures of the universe deserve a chance...that all have the goodness inside." He put his hand on Grandma's shoulder. "Is this man not such a creature as this?"

Grandma scowled at Tate. "He's a creature, all right."

I looked at Amy. "If your dad took the job, you'd be able to stay here." Amy nodded, a hopeful smile forming on her lips. I turned to Grandma. "She loves it here, Grandma. Not just Forest Grove, but your place. *Especially* your place."

Grandma looked at Amy, and then at Mr. Harnox, and finally me. "Looks like I'm outvoted," she said.

Then she took a deep breath and turned her gaze on the ex-sheriff. "Two conditions, Tate," she said finally. "One, there will be absolute *no* scaring or harassing my guests. Do you understand?"

Tate shrugged, then nodded.

"Good. Two, my grandson is leaving soon, and I need more help. I can't exactly advertise for the position. If you come on as head of security, then I'll need your daughter to take over his job."

Amy shrieked, "Really? Do you really mean it? "

"That's if you'd like the job, of course."

"I'd love it! Thankyouthankyouthankyou!" She grabbed Grandma in a bear hug and they spun around on the grass together, laughing. Amy beamed. "I have so many good ideas for this place. I can't wait to share them with you!"

Grandma cupped Amy's face in her hands. "I can't wait to hear them, dear."

Amy couldn't stop smiling. She hugged me now, crushing me against her. I glanced at Tate. He raised an eyebrow, but Commander Rezzlurr was already pulling him toward the spacecraft. "Would you like a tour of my ship, officer? She's a top-of-the-line model."

Tate turned to follow the commander. "Don't mind if I do."

The green alien wrapped his arm around Tate's shoulders and gestured broadly toward the ship. "You'll love this baby. She's a full traveling precinct, and more. Got an extensive armory and a maximum-security jail. Plus a state-of-the-art hospital and enough food and water to last us years. The next time—"

Tate stopped. "Amy, would you like to come with us? This is the kind of thing you'd probably like to see, am I right?"

"Yessss! Thanks, Dad. I'd love to." She turned to me. "And thank you, Scrub, for the best summer ever."

Her face was so excited, I couldn't help but smile back at her. "You're welcome. And I kind of think that I'm going by *David* now."

"Sounds good to me," she said, and then she kissed me right in front of everyone.

She stepped back and looked at me, her eyes shining. Tate might have been scowling at me, but I didn't look, I didn't even care. I exhaled, and it felt like the first time that I had really done so since the night of the mob. Everything was going to be okay—Grandma would be back in business, and Amy got to stay and learn about aliens firsthand.

But as Amy smiled at me, I also felt a wave of sadness wash over me. Everything might be great . . . but I wouldn't be here to enjoy any of it. I knew it was selfish to feel that way, but I couldn't help it. I tried to push those feelings underneath and just be happy for them.

Amy squeezed my hand one more time before she dropped it and followed her dad. "Bye, David!" she said over her shoulder, and then raced to join Tate. He was walking beside Commander Rezzlurr, who continued his orientation as they made their way to the ship. "Now, the most important part of your job will be spotting outlaw aliens. If anyone busts out of prison, they usually look to hole up on a primitive planet before we can get the transporters shut down. We need you to . . ." His voice trailed off as the trio disappeared into the humongous craft.

There were only three of us left on the lawn. Mr. Harnox gave Grandma a hug. "Thanks to you for everything and all," he said. "I am thinking to follow their steps."

"You are?" she said.

"Yes. I recognize this spaceship. These police travel nearby to my planet. I will ask them to give me the hitchhike ride."

Grandma smiled, her eyes getting misty. "You get to go home," she said.

Mr. Harnox nodded and returned her smile. "Thanks to you for welcoming me so much to your Earth. I travel oftentimes, and you are the most kind and generous creature I am meeting."

"Thank you, dear."

"Would you think it possible for me to return one day?"

"That would be lovely."

They hugged again, and then Mr. Harnox shook my hand. "Good-bye, little man. Thanks to you, as well."

"Thanks for being so good to Grandma," I said. "And for playing hoops with me."

Mr. Harnox grinned and put his hands over his head, like he was playing defense. I mimed dribbling a basketball and spun into him, flipping up that sweet little half-hook shot. "He shoots, he scores!" I cried. Mr. Harnox laughed and clapped his long gray hands together. "That move is going to help win me the starting point-guard spot this fall, I can feel it. Thanks again." The tall gray alien held his hand out, and this time I wasn't weirded out at all about shaking it. "Bye, Mr. Harnox."

"Good-bye."

He walked away and entered the spaceship. Grandma and I stayed out on the lawn, watching it.

Grandma turned to me. "Are you okay, David?" I nodded. I didn't trust myself to talk. Grandma searched my face. "What's wrong?"

I shrugged. "I just . . . I'm really going to miss this place, you know?"

"We'll miss you too, of course, but you'll be back."

"What do you mean?"

"You're coming back next summer, aren't you?"

"Would that be okay?" I said. "I mean, you've got two employees now. Are you . . . are you sure you want me?"

Grandma put her hands on my shoulders. "What if there's another emergency? I've never met anyone as resourceful as you. We need you here. I want you to visit whenever you feel like it." She smiled. "In fact, even if you don't feel like it, you'd still better come back. You hear?"

A weight lifted off my chest. I gave her a hug. "Thanks, Grandma."

Grandma gazed up at the giant spaceship. But I looked back at the Intergalactic Bed and Breakfast. The house was a portal to spectacular destinations all across the universe.

But of all the billions of places it led to, I had found the one I liked the most.

EPILOGUE

I sat in the airport terminal and slid my laptop out of my carry-on bag. There was a two-hour delay for my flight home, and I intended to enjoy every minute of the first Internet connection I had picked up in over two months.

When I reached in my bag to pull out the battery pack, a white envelope dropped out. I opened it up and grabbed the note that was inside.

Dearest David,

I realize now that we never discussed the salary for your unique summer job. I took all of the alien currency from the drawer in your room, and I will give it to the trader the next time he comes by. Using his exchange rate, I have enclosed a check that I think comes close to the correct sum.

I will miss you every day. Please send your old grandmother a letter every now and again. I will make sure to keep your bedroom ready for your return.

Until then, may the celestial lights of the cosmos serve as a nightly reminder of all the new friendships that you have forged this summer.

Intergalactically yours,

Grandma

I fished a cashier's check out of the envelope and unfolded it. Then I almost dropped it on the ground. That was a *lot* of zeroes.

When I finally finished imagining all of the things I could buy with my summer-job money, I folded up the check and stuffed it in the secret compartment in my wallet. Then I went back to the computer.

I scrolled through my Favorites list—some sports message boards, a few comedy sites. But...they seemed kind of boring. I realized that I hadn't missed them too much after all.

So I went to my e-mail account. I deleted all of the junk and found one real e-mail.

Hey there,

Just got back into Tampa and I'm glad you're coming home. It'll be great to see you again. You'll get into town a few days before your mom, and I think that's a good thing. You and I have a lot to talk about, and I think it's probably best if we do so privately, at least at first. Maybe we could drive over to Orlando and talk on the way. Or would you rather just shoot hoops in the backyard while we

catch up? It's up to you. Either way, it will be good
to spend some time together.

See you soon,

Dad

Yes, it *would* be good to see him. I have a feeling we won't
have trouble cutting through the small talk from here on out.
I started a new e-mail message.

Hey Tyler,

You know what that bitter taste is in the back
of your throat? No? Let me tell you. It's the taste
of DEFEAT. That's right, because I'm the guy who
won the Colossal Summer Challenge. Now you know
what it feels like to

I stopped typing as memories of that night in the woods
came back to me. Now that everything was fixed at Grandma's, I could focus on the good parts. It was one of the best
moments of my life. Everything had been perfect. (Except
for, you know, the escaping aliens.)

I hit DELETE. That moment was for me and Amy alone.
I started again.

Hey Tyler,

Flying today—be home late tonight. I'll give you
a call tomorrow. We should hang out. There's still a
couple of days left before school starts, right? And
speaking of school, I think we should stop making

fun of the Sci-Fi/Fantasy Club guys this year.
Maybe they're on to something with

I hit DELETE again. Tyler was never going to change. I
would just have to make my own decisions at school, and
if he didn't like them...well, I'm pretty sure I could make
new friends.

> Hey Tyler,
> I didn't get to play much ball this summer. But
> guess what? It doesn't matter. I'm still taking that
> starting point-guard spot. You might have gone
> to all of the camps and tournaments, but Coach
> said he's looking for leadership. I'm guessing you
> didn't pick much of that up hanging out at the pool
> all summer, staring at Amanda Peterson and her
> friends. My advice? Next summer, get a job.
> See you on the court,
> David

I smiled and hit SEND.

ACKNOWLEDGMENTS

Whenever I used to read the Acknowledgments section I would always think: Why does this author have such an incredibly long list of people to thank? Isn't writing pretty much a solitary activity?

Then I tried to write a book and get it published. So here is my incredibly long list of people I'd like to thank:

My parents, for not making their overly imaginative little boy feel weird whenever they caught him talking to himself in his bedroom as he was making up stories. (And, you know, sort of acting them out and doing the hand gestures and whatever.)

My first readers, Myra "(*sniff*) I'm so proud of you, honey" Smith and Tyler "Ummm . . . what's with all the Narnia stuff?" Robbins, for being with me since the first day of this crazy adventure.

My daughters, Logan and Cameo, for all of the laughter and cuddles. And for occasionally staying out of my writing room. And also for barging into my writing room and jumping on my lap and totally interrupting me. I need that sometimes.

My entire extended family for all of the support. My patron saints, Ginger and Carter; and babysitters extraordinaire Cindy and Joe, GG, and the Johnson clan (Brian, Cameo, Finnigan, Clayton, and Barrett).

My friend Sam, a great librarian, for the book recommendations and good times.

Award-winning author Terry Trueman, whose amazing writing skill is surpassed only by his generosity and kindness.

My agent, George Nicholson, for the best piece of advice I've ever received. Also Erica Silverman, Marcy Posner, Ira Silverberg, Kelly Farber, and everyone at Sterling Lord Literistic.

To Jacqueline Byrne and Leah Hoyer, the first people to show professional interest in my work. Your encouragement meant so much to me.

Everyone at the MFA in Writing for Children and Young Adults program at VCFA, especially my advisors Uma Krishnaswami, Margaret Bechard, and Martine Leavitt; the folks in my first workshop; and my fellow Sweet Dreams and Flying Machines (thanks for the speed-editing at rez, Jessica, Linden, and Mima!).

Amazing author Rita Williams-Garcia, who helped so much with this story during my first semester (and kept a straight face when I told her what I would be working on).

My writing buddy, the fine children's author Royce Buckingham, for talking shop over the lunch combo special at the House of Orient.

Film agent Jody Hotchkiss, for excellent editorial advice and a ton of support, along with the whole team at Hotchkiss and Associates.

Producers David Hoberman, Todd Lieberman, and Albert Page. For liking aliens.

The great team at Disney-Hyperion Books for Children and Disney Publishing Worldwide, including Jeanne Mosure, Hallie Patterson, Jennifer Levine, Jennifer Crowell, and Tyler Nevins.

My wonderful editor, Stephanie Owens Lurie. For everything. I feel like the cover of this book should read "By Clete Barrett Smith and Stephanie Owens Lurie." (Does every writer feel that way? Or just the lucky ones?)

Most important, I'd like to thank you. If you bought this book, or got it from the library, or borrowed it from a friend, or stole it from an enemy, or downloaded it, or rescued it from molding in someone's garage—however you got your hands on it—I thank you. I'm thrilled to share my story with you.

(Wait, I almost forgot. What is the opposite of thanking? Cursing? If so, then curse you, viral videos and online Scrabble. Curse you for wasting so many of my writing hours. Never again shall I let your charms lull me into a completely nonproductive trance. You know, starting tomorrow.)

Book 2

Alien on a Rampage

by Clete Barrett Smith

1

When the taxi pulled up to Grandma's place, I opened my door before the driver had even come to a complete stop. "Whoa, buddy, take it easy," he said. "You'll get there on time—it's not going anywhere."

Then he parked at the curb and got a good look at The Intergalactic Bed and Breakfast. His mouth dropped open, forming a circle that matched his wide eyes. I guess some people just aren't used to seeing a huge Victorian-style house covered in a mural of swirling galaxies, with silver spaceship sculptures jutting up all over the front yard. Especially at the edge of a forested wilderness on the outskirts of a tiny Pacific Northwest town.

"Ummm...okay...on second thought, that place looks like it could blast off any minute. I guess you better hurry up."

I hopped out of the taxi, pulling my suitcase off the backseat. "Thanks for the ride," I said, handing the driver a wad of cash through his open window. "See you again in a couple of months." The driver nodded and collected the money but kept his eyes fixed on the house.

Jogging along the white picket fence, I thought about how different this was from my arrival last summer. Back then, the only thing I had to worry about was starting seventh grade in the fall. But that was before Grandma had given me my summer job and put me in charge of defending the biggest secret on the planet.

I stopped at the front gate and took in the view. I had been a little worried that things might've changed since I was last here. But everything looked to be in the right place, just the way I remembered it.

Well, okay, maybe not the *right* place. Grandma's house could only be in the right place if it was hosting a Klingon birthday party on one of Jupiter's outer moons. But it looked the same as last summer, and that was good. Seeing it again felt like coming home.

But as I looked up at the porch...I don't know, I guess I felt a little disappointed. It's not like I'd expected a big WELCOME BACK! banner and a marching band playing under a blizzard of confetti. But maybe I had expected *something*. Maybe someone sitting on the front porch, waiting for me.

Maybe Amy. I mean, I'm pretty sure she knew I was flying in today.

No big deal. This would give me a chance to surprise them. If I had planned it better, I could have brought an alien disguise and mingled with the dinner crowd in the dining room, to see how long it took Grandma to figure out I was there with the rest of her customers. But I'd have to settle for sneaking in through the back door and catching someone off guard.

I left my suitcase just inside the gate and darted between the spaceship sculptures for cover. When I reached the side of the house, I ducked, and crept below the first-floor windows, making my way to the back. As I tiptoed up the back porch stairs, I heard someone rustling around in one of the sheds behind me.

Perfect. I could sneak up and startle them, and then we'd laugh about it . . . unless it was Sheriff Tate. I mean, "Head of Security" Tate, or whatever his official title was, now that he was working here. Last summer I had devised a secret plan to humiliate him in front of the entire town. But only because he had led everyone in Forest Grove to the front lawn of the bed-and-breakfast, threatening to storm the place and drag Grandma's customers off to jail, or worse.

So it was probably not a real good idea for me to give that guy another big surprise. Ever.

The door to the shed stood partially open, and someone was kneeling on the ground, hunched over a scattering of spare parts. The carcasses of an old computer, a lawn mower, and a carpenter's nail gun rested against the far wall.

It looked like pieces had been stripped from all three and mashed together to form the device in the center of the shed.

I crept forward for a better look. The figure inside the doorway was wearing a pair of black coveralls. A pale hand punched a string of numbers into the computer's keyboard. Instantly the blade from the lawn mower whirred to life and rose in the air, a mini helicopter propeller. Attached below was a sheath of tubing that held a cartridge of nails. The gadget hovered in the air in the middle of the shed.

The figure in coveralls grabbed the computer's mouse and whipped it back and forth, clicking furiously at the button. The floating thing rotated in the air and spat out a machine-gun stream of nails.

I heard a noise over the whirring of the blades. It might have been laughter, but it was so harsh it almost sounded like someone choking. I had a pretty good idea this wasn't Grandma or Amy. Or anyone who called Earth home. Not even Tate.

I looked up and saw paper targets spread across the walls of the shed. Although the device had only been in action for a few seconds, each target had at least a dozen nails slammed through its bull's-eye. The nails were sunk into the wood all the way to their heads.

Bzzzzt! Sparks shot from the computer's mainframe, where the casing had been cracked open to expose the circuit boards. It sizzled, and the smell of burning plastic was awful. The figure in the coveralls shouted, "Curse these cave dwellers and their primitive toys!" just before the flying device spun out of control and smashed into a wall. The wreckage crashed to the ground in a smoky heap.

"Whoa." I barely breathed the word, but the being on the ground jumped up as if he'd been electrocuted. He stepped out of the shed and slammed the door.

Then he turned and loomed over me. His skin was bone white and smooth all over, making his head look like a skull. The dark purple lips and black eyes didn't help much. I stumbled backward and almost fell onto the grass.

But I recovered quickly. Sure, it had been almost a year since I had seen an alien, but you only had to remember they were pretty much just like us inside. Even the really creepy-looking ones. "Hey, sorry if I startled you," I said.

His upper lip contorted into a sneer, revealing sharp teeth. "You are equipped with neither the cognitive capacity nor the physical dimensions necessary to alarm one such as myself." He made a shooing motion with the back of his hand. "Now return to your little village of like-minded dirt-crawlers."

Yikes. First, no welcoming committee—and now this? I stared at him for a moment before I could even muster up a response. "Oh, no. I'm not from Forest Grove. I just got here from—"

"Your point of origin is irrelevant. Despite a few insignificant biological variations, humans are the same everywhere." The smile he gave me would have looked fake and condescending on any planet. "My meaning—and here I shall speak very slowly to aid your limited comprehension—was that you should vacate the premises immediately. Your ultimate destination means little to me."

I took a deep, calming breath. Usually Grandma's customers were really nice, but occasionally you came across a rude one. And then you had to remember the best thing about meeting them at a bed-and-breakfast: they would be gone in a day or two. "You know, you're not in a very good mood for someone on vacation." I tried to keep my tone light; it would kind of spoil my arrival if I got into a big argument with a Tourist before I had even seen Grandma.

He drew back and made a face like he had just noticed that my clothes were made of flaming manure. "Vacation?" he said. "You presuppose that I would choose to spend even one moment here of my own free will?"

What was this guy's problem? "Well...you're here, right? And this is a popular vacation spot for those who are, you know"—I leaned in and whispered so he would know that I was in on Grandma's secret—"*like you*."

The alien cleared his throat. "There exists no one in this pathetic little galaxy who is"—he leaned in and did an impression of my voice that was very unflattering and highly accurate—"*like me*." He straightened back up. "And certainly you did not say *popular*?" The alien scoffed so forcefully it sounded like he was hawking up a big wad of phlegm. "Your species' affinity for self-delusion is appalling."

Okay, so I might not have known what some of those words meant, but I could tell he was trying to insult me. And probably everyone I've ever met. But I remembered my training from last year. No use in getting mad. Time to just start over. "Look, I think we got off on the wrong foot, with my sneaking up on you. Sorry about that." I stuck out my hand. "I'm David. I'll be working here this summer."

"Oh, I have managed to deduce that all by myself at this point in the conversation." He glanced at my hand distastefully. "There actually exist a few of us in the universe who put our brains to more use than obsessing over matters of fancy and trivia. You must be the visiting earthling child, two generations removed from the proprietor here."

I dropped my hand. Despite how rude the alien was acting, I was kind of glad that Grandma was apparently excited enough about my visit to mention it to one of her customers. "Right. So, I'm David. And you are...?"

"Your barely evolved vocal mechanism could not begin to pronounce my true name."

I noticed the lettering stitched above the pocket on his coveralls. "So...I should just call you 'Bob,' then?"

His black eyes narrowed into slits. Little gray spiderweb lines appeared on his throat, creeping out of his collar and up his neck. They looked like cracks in his skin. "If a cockroach could insult a king, then I might be offended by that comment."

I couldn't help but snort a little. Maybe this is what passes for humor on the Planet of the Sarcastic Skull-Faces. I figured that since I wasn't officially on the clock yet, there was really no need to try to get along with this guy anymore. Soon he would step into one of the transporters and get beamed back home. Maybe somebody there would be willing to listen to his anti-human tirades.

"See ya," I said.

I started to turn away, but he stepped toward me. "The average life span of a human is laughably brief." He glanced up at the house, checking the windows, and then leaned in close. Two small red dots glowed in the center of his black eyes. The spiderweb lines turned darker and reached up past his jaw line. He whispered, "If you ever sneak around and try to catch me unawares again, yours will be much shorter than average."

The look in those eyes totally freaked me out. But I forced myself to stare right back at him. "Don't worry about it," I said. "We'll probably never see each other again."

"How I wish that were true." The crack lines on his skin faded, and his face was smooth and white again. He pulled on a cap that matched his workman's coveralls. "It is the great shame of my existence to admit that we are fellow employees at the moment."

My mouth fell open. "Fellow employees?"

The alien sighed heavily. He looked straight up and addressed the sky. "Why must these humans repeat everything as if the veracity of a statement will be altered somehow through its repetition?"

"Fellow employees?" I said again. I couldn't believe this. Any of this.

He looked back down at me. "Yes, that's right. Say it a few more times and you might just get it." He leaned even closer. "But here is something I shall only say once. Tell no human of the circumstances of our meeting here. And stay as far away from me as possible."

He straightened back up and marched away, along the side of the house and up the steps to the porch out front.

I just stared after him. I don't think I blinked for over a minute. This was definitely not how I had imagined my arrival.